The LIGHT in EVERYTHING

KATYA BALEN

BLOOMSBURY
CHILDREN'S BOOKS
LONDON OXFORD NEW YORK NEW DELHI SYDNEY

BLOOMSBURY CHILDREN'S BOOKS
Bloomsbury Publishing Plc
50 Bedford Square, London WC1B 3DP, UK
29 Earlsfort Terrace, Dublin 2, Ireland

BLOOMSBURY, BLOOMSBURY CHILDREN'S BOOKS and the Diana logo
are trademarks of Bloomsbury Publishing Plc

First published in Great Britain in 2022 by Bloomsbury Publishing Plc
This edition published in Great Britain in 2023 by Bloomsbury Publishing Plc

A catalogue record for this book is available from the British Library

ISBN: HB: 978-1-5266-2299-0; PB: 978-1-5266-2298-3;
TPB: 978-1-5266-4740-5; eBook: 978-1-5266-2301-0;
ePDF: 978-1-5266-5094-8

2 4 6 8 10 9 7 5 3 1

Typeset by RefineCatch Limited, Bungay, Suffolk

Printed and bound in Great Britain by CPI Group (UK) Ltd, Croydon CR0 4YY

To find out more about our authors and books visit www.bloomsbury.com
and sign up for our newsletters

For Lucy Mackay-Sim,

who is always right

Praise for

The LIGHT in EVERYTHING

'This is Balen's best book yet: ambitious, funny, spirited, moving, heartfelt and bold all at once. She's a force to be reckoned with'

Ross Montgomery

'I loved this book. The deftness with which Katya creates such passionate, funny, broken, brave characters. What an achievement. Katya Balen can break your heart and make you snort with laughter in the same sentence'

Natasha Farrant

'This story literally took me by storm. A brave heart-dive into the deep emotions of Tom and Zofia, it's beautifully told with care and tenderness'

Jasbinder Bilan

'I loved this book!'

Hilary McKay

‘A bold, bright story of blended families, and how two remarkable children cope when their lives change dramatically. Katya Balen’s writing fizzes with her trademark originality and voice. This is another stunningly good read from one of my favourite authors’

Emma Carroll

‘Katya Balen is rapidly becoming one of my favourite writers. This is a beautiful book that will capture you from the first page. An incredible book by an incredible writer. I loved it’

Lisa Thompson

‘A sensitive story about stitching a new family together from frayed pieces. So vividly imagined you can taste the salt in the air’

Aisha Bushby

‘Original, compulsive, uplifting: this is another triumph for Balen’

The Times

Books by Katya Balen

The Space We’re In

October, October

The Light in Everything

ZOFIA

I was born in a storm. The sky cracked with lightning and thunder shook the sea. The rain lashed the cliffs and it was like the whole world had tipped upside down and the ocean was falling from the sky. The weather was furious and so was I. The midwife said she'd never seen such an angry baby and in all the photographs I am a red-faced ball of fury and my fists are clenched and my mouth is a shouting *O*. I sometimes feel like that storm blasted its way into me. That's what Dad says too when I'm being loud and rowdy and raucous and shouty. Which is a lot of the time apparently. But I feel a spark and rumble inside me and it's like the storm is stretching itself and waking up. Sometimes it goes back to sleep. And sometimes it really doesn't. And that's when Dad says things get *turbulent*.

Dad and I are a pair. Two peas in a pod. Two halves of a whole. Two guinea pigs in a hutch. I once read that you can't ever have one guinea pig because it'll be so lonely that it might die. In Switzerland it's actually illegal. I can't imagine being sent to prison and locked up day and night because you only had one guinea pig but I guess that's what happens. Anyway even though guinea pigs will die of loneliness, if you try to introduce a new guinea pig into the hutch then the other one will attack it and probably bite its head off or something. I'm happy with a dog and a cat.

Dad and I like most of the same stuff. Well, he doesn't like very loud music or wearing gold Doc Martens or eating twenty Oreos in a row but he loves the sea and jokes and watching really really bad TV and spicy food and graphic novels. And he might actually like Oreos but he's never quick enough to find out.

Dad and I live in a cottage with sloping stone walls and a bright yellow front door and a front garden full of every wild flower in existence ever. If you look out of the windows or stand in the garden or just look up then you can't just see the sea but you can hear it and smell it and sometimes you can taste it too.

Our cottage looks like something out of a picture book. It has roses around the door that I used to make spells and potions with when my best friend Dommo and I were little, and it has a winding path up to its yellow door. It's the kind of cottage from that kind of book where you see a mum and a dad and a little girl and maybe a dog that can fetch slippers and it's a perfect little life. And that's what it's like. Well, we have the dog but he's more likely to eat slippers than fetch them and Mum died when I was a baby but otherwise it's exactly what it's like.

I wouldn't change a thing about our lives right now.

TOM

The dark around me is filled with light. That's what I tell myself. There is the acid orange glow of a street lamp just beyond the curtains. There is the gentle spill of yellow melting on to the carpet from under my bedroom door. There is the slow red eyeblink of a charger plugged into the wall opposite.

But the space around me is stained with soot and ink and shadows. The shadows slink and twist and reach and grasp. They slither and slip into something new and their edges blur and stretch. My fingers twitch. I gulp lungfuls of dirty dark air. Try to slow my breath and push away the black. Be my own light. My heart is clawing in my chest. I count the shapes I can see.

One. Two. Three.

The shadows that creep and swirl on the walls are nothing but shapes. Just a collection of angles and lines bound together by black. Shapes can't hurt you. They're nothing. The dark can't hurt you.

Four. Five.

But what's hiding in it can.

Six.

My heart is on fire.

I reach out in the blacknothing that swoops around my face like the flap of a bat and flip the emergency switch next to me.

Light.

Light streams and pours and floods. Light swallows the darkness whole and shrinks it backwards into scraps that only flicker in the corners. Light splinters through the glass prisms that sit on my desk and the walls are a dance of rainbows. I stop counting seconds and count the colours instead. I run through them like the names of friends. I race through the syllables.

Redyellowgreenblueindigoviolet.

Redandyellowandgreenandblueandindigoandviolet.

Red and yellow and green and blue and indigo and violet.

My heartbeat slows a little to something that isn't a dull howl against my ribs.

I tap the clock on my bedside table and it glows. So does the liquid light in my lava lamp. I have six different types of light in my room.

I made it one minute and thirteen seconds without it.

I get out a piece of square paper and I fold it. I follow the lines my fingers know and I don't even have to think about the shapes I'm making. My heartbeat starts to match the slow and careful turns and by the time I finish the paper star everything is in rhythm again.

I pull the duvet up to my chin and turn to face my lava lamp. When I close my eyes, there's no darkness but instead illuminations painted on my lids like fireworks.

In the morning before school the sun is hung in the sky and the darkness only scurries in corners.

I stand where the waves first start to lick the shore. I'm barefoot and I wriggle my toes to make prints in the sand that the sea rushes hungrily to fill. In seconds it can be like I wasn't even there.

I run at the waves and slip beneath them like a fish. The water and the light turn me to silver. The sea roars in my ears and crashes against the sand and salts my skin. I tumble and turn and twist underneath a slick blanket that covers a whole new world. Puffs of silver fish dart through my toes and ribbons of seaweed dance around my ankles. When I burst through the surface and breathe in the sky again I feel like a whole fresh new Zofia. The salt and the spray scrubs away any aches or worries that were starting to drumbeat inside me.

My babcia in Poland always wanted me to have a

baptism and Mum and Dad said no when I was a tiny baby, but maybe she'd like me doing this even though it's probably not quite the same. But any time I feel like my anger or annoyance or even a stupid little mouse-peek of loneliness might be getting too big then I run down from the house to the beach and let the salt wash it all away. I can see the sea from my bedroom window. I can hear it and smell it too. I used to say it was my friend and even though I'm old enough now to know that the sea can't be your friend I still sort of think it somehow.

I tread water. In the distance blurred against the dark sky is my number-one nemesis. Dommo said it was a ridiculous name for a yawning mouth of rocks biting and chopping against the waves. Fiji. It's called Fiji because Fiji is beautiful and tropical and in the middle of a warm blue sea and this is not. I think this is meant to be funny but I'm not sure I get it. Anyway people call it Fiji and so it's called Fiji. And it's my nemesis. This is the year I'll defeat it. I'll swim far enough to stand on top of it and bellow into the sky. I'm going to swim every single day, and every single day I'll get a bit faster and a bit stronger and a bit closer.

When I am scrambling out of the water I hear Dommo's voice. She's laughing her Dommo-laugh which is like a hyena crossed with an albatross. It always makes me laugh too. Then I hear Halima. I blink the sand and wind away from my eyes.

Dommo is carrying a large shape. I squint and she unfurls it and starts to run. The wind picks it up and throws it high in the air. A bird-shaped kite dances in the sky.

Dommo is flying a kite. With Halima. Without me. The wind roars in my ears and a hurricane starts to spin inside me.

Dommo spots me and waves. She's shouting something but the wind whips away her words. She staggers towards me and the kite bucks and dips like a furious horse. I want to do that too. I want to rage into the swirl and swoops of the wind. I want to twist myself in the air and howl. She didn't want me here and I am being left out. Dommo and I do everything together. Just like me and Dad.

Dommo finally makes it over to me and she's still grinning and she says *we knocked at yours but you weren't in obviously because you're in the sea do you want a go* and I feel a rush of relief that lifts me higher than the wind ever could.

TOM

Mum can't always pick me up from school. She works shifts as a hospital doctor. Everyone else in my class just walks home. It would be a lot easier if I could do that too and I know that. But I can't. Walking home isn't as bad as sitting in the dark but coming back to an empty flat in the fading winter light might be worse. So I sit in afterschool club and I don't talk to anyone and they don't talk to me.

The worst shifts are the ones when she's gone for the night. When that happens Mrs Adams from the flat below us comes to stay. She is gentle and kind but she turns my light off at 8 p.m. When I turn it back on she doesn't like it and tells me I'll never get enough sleep to grow up big and strong. I try to tell her that I'll never get any sleep at all if I'm stuck in the pitch dark and shadows are creeping all around me and wrapping themselves around my skin. But she doesn't listen and she clicks the light off every time and plunges me back in time. Back to before.

The sea is cold today. I don't go in. The waves are frosted and the sky is furious and rain-filled. Even in a wetsuit I would turn blue. I need a plan, because it's only going to get colder.

I turn the taps on cold and fill the bath until water spills over the sides and rushes away through the cracks in the floorboards. I plunge my hand in and swirl so that the water starts to wave and whisper like the sea.

I put on my wetsuit, get Dad's old plastic stop-watch and get in. It's so cold that my teeth chatter and my legs tremble even though I'm not asking them to do anything. I am burning with the fire of the ice-cold water. I take deep breaths that slow my wild heart and I clench my jaw and I go under.

One. Two. Three.

My eyes are open and the world above is soft through the ripples.

Four. Five. Six.

My lungs are full and empty and my skin is electric.

Seven. Eight. Nine.

The cold is shooting arrows in my blood.

Ten. Eleven. Twelve.

I need air I need air I need air. Thirteen.

I burst through the surface of the water and swallow great mouthfuls of air and I feel it racing through my blood.

Thirteen seconds is pathetic. I dry off and write the number down in an old notebook. I'll do better tomorrow.

TOM

Last night I made thirteen paper owls in the bright lights of my room before I could fall asleep. I put them in the cardboard box that's a spill of bright folded paper.

I have to fold paper and focus to stop my hands trembling. Every night is the same. The nights are the worst because I am so afraid of the creeping darkness and it's when my thoughts are loudest. The ones that tell me I'm not safe. The ones that curl like smoke and whisper that we might be happy now but it won't last. That it never lasts. That he won't stay away.

In the morning light it's easier to breathe those thoughts away. I can tell myself that Dad can't come back to get us now. I can tell myself everything is OK. I can tell myself that I wouldn't change a thing about our lives right now.

I have apologised a thousand times for the state of the bathroom and listened to about a million *wet floorboards will rot and the cat will fall throughs*. I have also managed sixteen seconds in the strange submerged bathtub world. I write it down and then go to the cold beach to let the floorboards dry a bit.

The beach is wild. The wind is tearing the water like paper and there is white confetti scattered on the waves. The sea is wild too and it's mine. I can feel the salt spray curling my hair and speckling my skin. I look at Fiji and I can see its raggedy flags whipping in the wind. Some of them are bright even in the dim light. Some of them are so faded they flicker and then blend into the sky around them. Some of them have been there since before I was born. Since before Dad was born. Since before Babcia, which is Polish for

Grandma, was born. Since before Pra Babcia, which is Great-grandma in Polish, was born.

Most of the really old flags have been whipped away by storms or dissolved by salt spray or stolen by birds for their nests. But there are still hundreds of ripples of fabric like rainbow waves rising from the sea. And not one of them is mine. Three of them are Dad's and he told me once that it was the biggest and bravest thing he'd ever done. He'd just moved here from Poland and everything was strange and new but the sea was the same and he swam in it every single day and every single day he felt a little more like he was home here. He said he knew when he reached that rock he would be truly part of the sea and the sky and the cliffs and the sand and this new land. And when he got there it was the best feeling in the world except for when I was born. I want that feeling. I want him to see me standing on the rocks of Fiji and I want him to be proud.

I've got a deadline. Every year the oldest class at my little school spends a day before big school on the beach learning how to surf and sail and life-save and swim against the tide. It's like a beach party before we have to get the bus into town for lessons and before we're all split up into a million different classes. Our families get to come too. That's the day I show Dad how far I can swim and that's the day I'll put my flag on Fiji.

TOM

I love our flat. It is tiny but it's ours and it fits the two of us just right. We aren't allowed to paint it so it's all white but that's OK. We moved here two years ago when Dad went away for good. When he and Mum were together we lived in a house. Even though it had lots of rooms it never felt big because somehow he filled up every single centimetre and I shrank and shrank. I don't think I have ever unfolded myself properly until now. There were too many in-between places where we squashed into one cold grey bedroom and Mum would cry when she thought I was asleep and you could hear shouting through the walls. I stayed small and I stayed quiet but he found us anyway.

Here we put up colourful pictures and the sofa is red and squashy. We have a bathroom with framed drawings on the wall that I did when I was little and somehow Mum saved even when we had to leave everything else behind. I think she kept them at work.

The flat has a kitchen in miniature but I chose bright orange pans and the fridge is full of my favourites and I can have them whenever I want. I have a little bedroom full of light and wires and paper. I can put my things exactly where I want them. I can leave them neatly on my desk and I know they'll be there when I get back.

Once Dad ripped up my paper birds. There were hundreds. I'd spent hours and hours on them and made each one with careful fingers. I thought maybe I could hang them from my ceiling and they would be bright in the dark. They were snow-white and they spilt in a perfect identical flock from my desk to my floor and they looked just ready to shake the paper from their wings and fly away. He screamed at me when he saw them. They were messy. They were for girls. They were pathetic. I was pathetic. He tore up every one until my carpet was a white sea of papery feathers. I hoovered up the remains and it felt like he'd killed them. That's when my fingers started trembling and the only thing that could make them stop was folding folding folding. But I didn't dare, so I shook and he shouted.

Dad and I walk along the beach path that winds its way up to our house. The sea is purple today. I try to skim a stone from where we're walking but the water is too far and the stone thumps uselessly on the sand. It was a good stone too. Perfectly flat and circular. I scramble on to the sand and trip over a tuft of heather and find it. When I scramble back again I am covered in damp sand and the side of my face itches from a heather scratch on my cheek. Dad rolls his eyes but he doesn't bother saying anything like I'm feral which I think is his favourite word for me. *If I'd known I was getting a wild animal, I'd have sent you back to the pet shop* is one of his favourite things to say to me and I always pretend to roar like a lion or beat my chest like a monkey or hiss like a snake.

Dad tells me a story about the sea as we walk. It's

an ancient legend from his pra babcia and it's about how if you are truly part of the sea and you understand its furies and its calmness and its salt and its spray and its depths and its shallows then you can wish upon the waves and it will come true. Pra Babcia wished for a pearl and the sea listened and the next morning an oyster was cracked open on the sand and in its belly was a shining moon. I say I would wish for a lifetime supply of Oreos and also the power of invisibility and also not to have to do fractions ever again. I ask Dad what he'd wish for but he doesn't answer and he's gazing at the white-hatted waves.

He seems distracted. His brain is quite often not really in his head. It's wandering off through hospital corridors and into patient files and into medicines and heartbeats. But he can snap back quick as a flash and pick me up and throw me in the sea or beat me at Uno in a whirlwind moment. But today even when I shout *race you* and our dog Pablo and I charge up the path at lightning speed it takes him forever and five minutes to shake off his big thoughts and chase us home.

TOM

Mum is late to collect me after a long day and after-school club is empty. I've been doing my English homework and I'm meant to be writing a story about a time you were a hero. You can make it up or it can be true. I'm making it up. In my story I'm going to be a superhero saving lives. But before every sentence I look at the minute hand clicking on the clock above the whiteboard and my superhero hasn't saved a single person. My page is a tangle of words that don't make sense. My heartbeat is a hummingbird thrum. My fingers are trembling. I start to fold the corners of my story into a bird.

She finally appears as a dark outline in the glass of the door. I know it's her even though she's just a shadow. The teacher in charge isn't very happy and she speaks sharply to Mum but relief is swooshing through me like cold water. I knew she wouldn't leave me. But I always worry about something happening. I always worry. When I was seven and we first left in a midnight moment I was so full of panic and cold that a seed of creeping fear planted itself in my spine and it never left. It spread its roots and grew and twisted around my bones until I didn't know where it ended and I began.

Mum doesn't seem worried though. She says she's really sorry and she lost track of time when she was having a quick coffee with someone from work and she gives my hand a squeeze and we walk home. Her cheeks are pink and her eyes are bright and she talks about her day in a way I haven't heard her talk for a long time. It's like there's colour in her voice again. Like she's happy. And I wonder what's made that happen.

I get up early and spend too long ducking and diving under the cold bath water, floating in the quiet rippled blue. I can feel the rubber balloon muscles of my lungs getting stronger and stronger.

Onetwothreefourfivesixseveneight

Heartbeat faster, lungs bursting

Nineteneleventwelvethirteen

Brain dizzy, water whirling

Fourteenfifteensixteenseventeen

I race through the last seconds until the edges of the world start to turn black. My chest burns and stars explode in my eyes as I sit up and check the stopwatch. It says 16:56 but everyone knows you round numbers up.

I write down seventeen seconds in my notebook and get dressed without even drying myself because

I am going to be very late. My clothes stick to my skin and itch.

At school I win at football, which is always five-a-side because there are only ten people in my class. My team is the red team and we win 5–2. I score two goals and I would have had a third if Jude hadn't fallen over his own feet right in front of me and made me fall over too and stain my knees grass-green. Miss Cassidy writes up the result on the board. Reds are in the lead by two matches this term. There's no official prize for the very official Ceto Class Football Tournament but I want to win anyway because winning makes me feel excellent.

After school we all go down to the beach even though it's October and the sunlight is being whittled away with every passing day. The sky is already blue-black and mottled with clouds. But the beach is always the most beautiful place in all of the whole wide world. Every day it's different. The half-moon of sand is cupped by cliffs sprayed green with heather and springy gorse. The sea and the sky are always dressed the same as each other, cloaked in grey velvet or blue silk or sparkling emeralds or darkest black obsidian or melted gold like treasure spilling from a chest. They stretch out lazily until they meet and then they push their edges together. Sometimes the line is hazy and sometimes it's pin-sharp. But they always meet. The sea has what Dad calls a mercurial temperament. He actually said something in Polish but we translated it together and then looked up the definition of the English word too because *mercurial* made as much sense to me as most Polish. Anyway it means it changes its mood on a whim and so do I. Sometimes everything seems calm but there's a storm rising. Halima and I had matching mood rings last year and hers was always a gentle roll of glittering blue-green to blushing pink and mine couldn't keep up with me. Maybe it was broken.

The sea is cold but I've been training my lungs and skin for this. I wriggle into my wetsuit behind a sand dune and plunge in head first. Dommo is standing on the shoreline with the stopwatch.

At first it's like the air has been punched from my lungs. But I remember from the bath that the feeling will pass and the burn will grow and twist and then it will turn into a low hum in the background of my body. When I start to feel stars whirling in my brain I roar through the surface and gulp in the sky. I keep swimming, my head bobbing. I kick and twist and my bones are liquid as I streak through the waves.

I feel part of the sea and I rise and fall with its breaths. It's better than winning at football.

When my legs start to scream I see how far I am. Closer than before. Not close enough.

Sixteen seconds crows Dommo and I'm disappointed but still lit up from my swim. I paddle back to the shore and play volleyball with Mo and Jacob and Jude, even though there are layers and layers of cold tunnelling through my skin.

We start to wander home when the cold is seeping through the sand and into our bones. The sea is beautiful black glass. I would stay later even though my teeth are chattering but Jacob and Jude, who are twins and always Jacob and Jude and never Jude and Jacob, have to get home for a piano lesson (do they share a piano at the same time and each play half is what I always want to know but in the goodbyes I always forget to ask) and Mo promised he'd build a rocket with his little sister. I try to get Dommo to stay with me but she says she has to be home for tea and so do I but I also want to stay on the darkening beach and watch the cliffs dissolve into the night. We scrabble up the sand and start to peel off in pairs. Dommo lives next door to me so we walk home together with the scent of the sea trailing behind us.

TOM

It's the weekend and I don't have anything to do, which is fine. Mum isn't here so Mrs Adams is watching TV in the living room and knitting some sort of cape. Usually when Mum isn't here on the weekends it's because she's working. This time it's different. She's on a date. When she told me I felt all of the blood in my head drop right down to my toes. I wanted her to laugh and mess my hair up and say she was joking. But she told me not to worry, as if those words might help. She told me where she'd be and she told me it was someone from work, but I still feel sick. Worry zaps in my brain because when it's just me and Mum we're safe.

It's raining outside and the sky is steel. Mrs Adams asks me if I'd like to go to the park but she's only asking to be kind. She looks relieved when I say I have a project to do for school. I don't. But I don't want to go to the park and pretend to have fun when really I'm looking through the misty light to see if he's there.

I make a tiny city. I make it out of paper. I fold everything carefully and make my lines and turns as straight and perfect as possible. I follow the instructions in the origami book exactly. I make skyscrapers. I make little houses. One is just for me and Mum. I make buses and a train and a boat for the river. I make a school for me. I make a hospital where Mum can work. I make everything just exactly as I'd want it to be and I make a big wall to keep us safe. The city spreads itself over my desk and the day slips away and my fingers aren't allowed to shake.

ZOFIA

It's Saturday and it's raining, which is about the most unfair thing in the whole wide world. I hate wet weekends. At first they're quite fun because we can light the wood burner and toast marshmallows and watch Netflix cartoons but after a while I am bouncing and itching and jumping to do something outside. But today it's so cold that my bones are icicles inside me when I stand in the front garden and look out across the beach. My breath plumes and I blow it out like a dragon. The sea is ink-black and the sand is grey and streaked with grubby ripples. Obviously it's still amazing but it's not quite as amazing as it is when it's spring or summer. I don't want to swim even though I need to practise. Even Pablo doesn't want to swim – he once stood outside for an hour in a snowstorm and refused to come in because he thought he'd seen a fox. It was actually an orange plastic bag but you can't tell him that. Mostly because he's a dog but also because he listens to precisely no one. I fill up the bath and plunge myself under the freezing surface for nineteen seconds and I am bouncy with triumph and the floor is soaked again.

But other than bath practice there's nothing to do today. Dad is out somewhere and he did say where but I wasn't listening. I'm meant to be at Dommo's house but we came back to mine instead because her little brother kept being a pest.

Dommo and I spend a few hours turning the stairs into an indoor toboggan slide. We do an excellent job using duvets and pillows instead of snow and an old tea tray and a cardboard box as toboggans. The cardboard box crumples on impact at the bottom of the stairs, so we've basically done a science experiment. The tea tray is much more successful so we share that and take turns to crash and whoosh and bang our way down the slope. It's the best possible way to spend a day when the light never made it through the clouds but plenty of rain did.

When Dad gets home the paintwork on the stairs and in the hall is very nearly exactly the same as it was before he left. Even so I am preparing my extremely convincing science experiment argument because the black mark above the bannister is particularly striking but he doesn't notice it. Which means something is very wrong. Dad notices everything. It is so unbelievably annoying. He'll notice if I'm wearing the same socks as the day before or if I've hidden my peas under my napkin or if I've spilt hot chocolate on a cushion and then turned it over so the wrong side is showing. Dommo grabs the pillows she borrowed-without-asking from her brother's bed and then shoots out of the back door quicksmart before Dad turns his eyes back on and sees the mark. It really is quite black. And big. And eye level.

But he doesn't. Instead he runs his hands through his hair like he always does when he's very tired and has worked a thousand hours or I've made him watch back-to-back Ghibli films or race me and Pablo along the beach against the wind.

He makes us sit down at the table.

He clears his throat.

He fiddles with his hair.

He twists his fingers together.

And just when I am about to get up and do something more interesting than watch him fidget he starts to speak. And I really wish he hadn't.

There's someone he wants me to meet.

There's never been someone he wants me to meet before.

He says it with the kind of voice that makes my nerves prickle with electricity. I don't like the way it feels at all.

I let him talk his way through all of his words and then I silently take Pablo to the sun-scattered beach. I throw my arms out wide and I let the wind rush through my fingers and I let it blow the feeling away.

There's a little tiny seed of worry stamping about in the back of my mind but I squash it down before it can start to shout. I stand on my windswept beach with my windswept hair and I watch the dying sun dust the sea with light.

TOM

I don't want Mum to have met anyone. The thought is neon-bright in my mind and I can't turn its colours off.

I wanted it to be just us. We have had two whole years of no Dad and nothing bad and I wanted everything to stay just where it was. It has taken me nearly those whole two years to believe he's not coming back and my brain still sometimes plays tricks on me. He always promised he would leave us alone and he broke that promise three times until he went away for good, so even when I knew he couldn't come for us I didn't feel safe. I want to keep Mum safe and I want to be able to live just how we want without worrying about what someone else might do. Mum used to worry so much about Dad and what he might do. She thought I didn't know but I did because

I could see every thought sketched on her face even when she thought she could keep them hidden. I know how much she stretched and shaped the things she did and said so that he would stay calm and not get angry.

Sometimes it worked.

Most of the time it didn't.

And now it could be just the same all over again.

I can't count any seconds in the dark tonight.

I walk Pablo along the curve of the beach. The wind is howling and it spits the sea and tangles my hair. Pablo is delighted. He is trying to stuff as much seaweed as possible into his mouth and it trails behind him as he runs, like some sort of gymnastic ribbon. Occasionally it trips him up and he rolls in a ball of weeds and paws and tail. He's going to be filthy by the time we get home. I'll let him into Dad's bedroom.

I leave Pablo to it and sit on the damp sand and watch the waves curling towards the shore. It's like the sea is breathing. I lean back so that my head crunches against the gritty ground and watch the feeble grey sky being swirled by the wind. That new strange feeling is growing shoots and leaves and I try to scream it away. I shout at the clouds and the noise bounces off the cliff and is whisked away by the wind and it's like I never made a single sound.

I don't want things to change.

TOM

We drive to a cafe. It takes quite a long time and I feel a bit green. When I get out of the car and drink great gulps of air it tastes like salt on my tongue. There are screeching cries circling above me and in the sky are a thousand gulls hunting for fish and chips. Their wings beat and graze the clouds and they bomb towards the waves chopping on the horizon. The sea makes me feel even greener. Mum gives me a smile and I swallow down the sick feeling but it's growing inside me and it's not because of the car journey.

I can see the girl and her dad sitting in the cafe and they look just like the photo Mum showed me when she told me that there were some people she'd like me to meet. Except in the photo the girl was smiling and stretched out in a star shape. Here she's curled up in a chair and furious.

Marek gets up straightaway as soon as we walk in and he leans forward like he's going to hug Mum but he stops and says *hello, Tom, I've heard so much about you, come and meet Zofia*. His voice has a lilt that sounds like the rise and fall of the waves outside. He is tall. Taller than Dad. I shrink back behind Mum and I go with her to get drinks instead of sitting down at the table with Marek and the glaring girl.

ZOFIA

When they arrive at the cafe and I meet that boy I thought Dad had made some sort of mistake when he told me how old he was. Eleven. Same as me except technically I'm a month older and I have a September birthday which means I'm nearly always the oldest in the class and now I'm nearly the oldest in the whole school. Anyway this boy looks like a Year 1. He is tiny and all stick arms and legs and huge eyes and dark hair that is way too long and nibbled-down nails. He is so pale he glows. His veins are bright blue rivers traced on skin and his bones jut so close to the surface that I wonder if they might break through and if they'd even stand out against the white of his arms. He looks like he is five or maybe six absolute maximum. Not even nine or ten and definitely not eleven. I can't tell if he is trembling or the slight breeze from the door is shaking his skeleton but I roll my eyes and I practise my best glare and my best snarl and I would give anything not to be right here.

I drink my hot chocolate and Tom sits in this terrified little meek silence and for every second he stays quiet I get louder and louder just to fill the space between us with something, with some noise and chatter and words so the weight of what is happening doesn't have a chance to settle around us. The louder I am the smaller he gets. He shrinks back into his chair until it's like he is made of liquid and will soon be smoke.

Fiona tries to talk to me about school and Pablo and swimming and she even mentions Ghibli films, which makes me realise Dad must have given her some sort of Official Zofia File. I growl and glower and turn myself into a storm. No one wants to talk to me when I'm a storm. I can be a quiet furious black cloud or I can be a raging tornado but the result is the same. But Fiona keeps trying and I am also trying very hard not to let the storm take over.

I cross my fingers tight and hope very hard that we never ever have to see them again. I don't often meet

Dad's girlfriends and never their children. This must be more serious than usual but that doesn't have to mean anything. I think and hope that after seeing the Incredible Shrinking Boy that Dad will realise it was all a completely mad idea and rethink things and we can go back to the cottage and it will be me and Dad and Pablo and Frida the cat and things will stay just the same as they were before.

But when we get home Dad has a massive go at me for being *rude* and *loud* and as soon as I hear those two words I drift away and grind them up to dust and spin myself into a space far away from shouting. I can't spin myself far away enough though and I can hear some words fizzing between us.

Important

special in our lives

this is serious, I want this to work out

please, Zofia.

But I whirl away and out of the door and I sit on the sand and I let the sound of the wind and the waves curl around me until I'm calm and I watch the flags in the distance dance for me.

TOM

The night after we meet Zofia and Marek for the first time I manage twenty-two seconds. I am trying so hard but the pictures I can see in the dark won't go away. My breaths are ragged. My fingers start trembling again. My muscles shiver. I am pathetic, just like he said I was. I start folding birds. Five. Ten. Fifteen. Twenty.

Mum said Marek isn't like Dad. She promised. But how can she know? Dad could be as normal as anyone. He'd turn up to parents' evening and he'd say loudly how brilliant my work was and all the teachers would smile. He'd take me and Mum out for pizza and tell the waiter *just treating my two best people in all the world, order what you like, guys, you're worth it*. He'd buy me expensive trainers that rubbed my feet raw even though I wore them every day.

I want it to just be us. The two of us. I don't want to worry about anyone else or have to flinch and shrink at every movement. I don't want to share our space. Our lives fit us perfectly now. I don't want to go back to feeling like everything is wobbly and unsafe. And that's exactly the feeling that's creeping back into my brain and shooting through my bones.

ZOFIA

Dommo and I stand on the shore and look out to Fiji. She keeps looking at her watch even though we know the time but it's a fancy waterproof thing her dad gave her for her birthday last week. She says we can use it to time our swims and measure them and time my underwater not-breathing or text whales or something. I don't need a watch to get me to Fiji. I just need to practise. I just need to swim.

We plunge into the water and it is so cold that it sets me on fire. It's a million times colder than the bath. Dommo actually screams. I hiss at her to shut up because we're not really meant to swim unless we tell an adult we're going to do it, but all that comes out is the *snap snap snap* of my chattering teeth. I take a breath that bumps its way down to my lungs through my trembling muscles and then I stick my head into the sea. The water makes everything in the whole world whirl away.

The waves push me back towards the shore. I beat against them with my arms and legs and try to push through the burning. I count in my head one and two and one and two and one and two for every stroke and the numbers start to run together. It's like fighting against a giant squid that keeps picking me up with a slippery tentacle and dropping me where I don't want to be. I turn my arms and legs under the crashing sea and I keep pushing forward but it feels like the weight of water is crushing my chest and I can't gasp enough air and I think that must be a jellyfish wrapping its moonlight body around me because my skin sings out.

I flip my feet and point my toes and I can still touch the grainy seabed, which is ridiculous because I must have been swimming for about three days so I can't possibly still be in the shallows. The moment I feel the sand on my feet the feelings dissolve out of me into the sea. I look over to Dommo and she's miles ahead of me and her elbows are dipping up and down as she swims further and further away.

I stamp back to shore and sit on the beach in my freezing wetsuit. I can swim. I can swim amazingly. I can swim better than everyone in Ceto including Dommo. I've been practising holding the air in my lungs and I've been practising fighting the shock of cold water. A roar of crossness starts to stretch in my chest. I hurl a smooth stone into the rushing waves and watch it crash through the water.

When Dommo finally makes it back to land she's blue-tinged and delighted. She looks at her stupid watch and tells me *that's a new record twenty minutes I think I'm nearly ready to do it what happened to you?* And I mutter something about a pulled muscle and squelch home for hot tea without her. I hate it when Dommo does stuff without me and even though we were doing it together technically, I was all by myself.

TOM

There is something new about Mum. Something lighter and it colours her movements and fizzes in her words. I feel like I am being torn in two. Like I am a piece of paper that has a careful neat line scored right down the middle then pulled apart. Two Toms. One of them wants Mum to be happy. And the other wants me to be happy. And I can't find a way to put the two pieces back together again.

We go out for a pizza just us two. We watch the chefs spinning the pizza dough in circles on their fingers and our eyes spin too until we're dizzy and laughing. I choose my favourite pizza which is extra cheese with mushrooms and I get a Coke as well. Mum doesn't like mushrooms so she calls me gross and I flick one at her and she doesn't tell me off because she knows it's a joke. If Dad were here I wouldn't have done it. As soon as I think that all the happiness whizzes out of me. When it's just me and Mum I can be myself and everything is OK.

ZOFIA

Every. Flipping. Weekend. Every single one. A thousand million weekends. A billion hours. All those wasted seconds and minutes and hours and days when I could have been practising in the waves, swimming through salt and storms and furious fish. Or still and quiet and breathless in the quiet of the bath, building up seconds and seconds of airlessness. I need it now more than ever, after that disastrous last swim, but every time I try in the bath I break through the surface gasping and choking and it's like I've forgotten how my body works. Anyway I also could have been playing volleyball with Ceto Class or video games with Dommo or making milkshakes with Halima and seeing just how many chocolate bars can fit in one standard blender. Instead we have to spend them with Tom and Fiona. We go bowling, which he hates and is rubbish at and the sound of the pins spinning makes him jump out of his skin. We go for pizza, which he picks at like a baby bird. We go to museums where he actually perks up a bit but I'm Bored with a capital B and maybe underlined too.

It's awful and I hate it and I hate them. Weekends used to be for indoor tobogganing and teaching Pablo to do backflips (so far unsuccessfully but then again I haven't had a lot of time for it lately) and messing about on the beach with Ceto Class. Now it's timetabled around trips and activities with the most boring boy on the planet.

Every time I complain to Dad he nods like he's listening and like he understands what it's like to be me and then he says *you need to go easy on Tom, he's had a really hard time* like that's my fault and like I can do anything about it. None of this is my fault.

Just before Christmas we go to the festive market in town. All four of us. Like some pretend happy family that someone threw together when they had their eyes closed. I wish I could go with just Dad and maybe Dommo. The air smells like sweet chestnuts and pine trees and there are stalls selling wooden boxes with secret compartments and glittering Christmas decorations and soft pink candyfloss shaped into stars. Dad buys Fiona a sparkling bauble traced with snowflakes for her Christmas tree and he kisses her cheek and whispers something I can't hear but I make a vomiting sound anyway and Tom looks appalled. Dad bats me on the head with a paper bag and Tom steps back and melts into Fiona's side.

He's so scared of everything. It's pathetic. I don't understand how one small boy can have so much to be terrified about. It makes me grind my teeth and clench my fists so tightly that my nails press half-moons into my palms.

I wander up to a stall selling gingerbread houses. Their roofs are dimpled and brightened with rainbow sweets and their windows are stained-glass sugar. I want one very very much and I turn to ask Dad if I can have some pocket money but he's not there. I spin round and in the whirl and blur of lights I see him and Fiona and Tom looking at a splash of Christmas stockings hanging from a stall. Just the three of them. No space for me to squeeze in between them. I stand and stare at them for a moment and I'm frozen. Then a toddler squeals somewhere and I unstick myself and shake my head from side to side. Dad says something to Fiona and she laughs into the darkening sky.

I bounce over behind them but no one sees me, so I lean forward until I'm close enough to see the freckles dusting the back of Tom's neck and I shout *BOO*.

And he jumps so much that he almost leaves his skin behind.

TOM

We don't see them every weekend but it's starting to creep up and up. At first it was once a month and then every three weeks. Now it's every two and sometimes once a week. It's a long drive between us so we take it in turns. We went to their cottage once and I met their dog and their cat who were both much nicer than Zofia even if the cat tried to swipe a paw at me and the dog nearly knocked me over when he said hello.

The Christmas market was the worst. Mum said Zofia didn't mean it and it was a misunderstanding. A mistake. A joke. She didn't know I'd leap and shake and cry. But I don't care. I hate her. I hate her loudness and her bounce and her rudeness and the way her voice rises above every other sound in the universe and settles in my brain. I hate the way she moves so quickly that I flinch. I hate the way she fills a room with her noise and her ideas. I hate the way she doesn't leave any space for me. I hate the way I feel around her. I hate the way Mum talks with her about swimming and films and dogs. I hate the way she's always there.

Most of all I hate the way when Mum tries to talk to Zofia she ignores her. Or she's rude and her words crush Mum and I can see the hurt starbursting in her eyes but she keeps trying. It reminds me of when she used to try and make Dad calmer and it never worked and all I want is for Mum not to have to do that any more.

But I push the feelings down and I fold them up like paper and I try to forget about Zofia.

ZOFIA

I spend my time underwater and I try to use the murky strangeness to wash away the thoughts in my brain but it doesn't work. I can't concentrate on holding my lungs still and they twitch and I cough and splutter and the seconds are wasted and ruined. I hate the way Fiona talks to me. Like I'm a little tiny child. Like I'm her child. Dad is always full of fury because I'm being *rude* and *unmanageable* but I don't want to answer one more single question about school or homework or the sea or films or dogs or anything at all because she is driving me up the wall and round the bend. I don't want to be her friend and I don't want a mother and I don't want her or Tom in my life at all. It's fine just me and Dad and Pablo and Frida. And maybe a pet tarantula because that's number one on my Christmas list even though Dad already said *absolutely not*.

TOM

At least we don't have to spend Christmas with them. That will be just me and Mum and the sparkling lights on the tree and we'll cook a meal together and we'll watch whatever TV we want without anyone telling us to turn it off or to clear up right away or to stop it stop it stop it. And maybe that will remind her that we don't need anyone else.

On Christmas Eve Mrs Adams gives me a tiny Christmas tree with little star bulbs dotted on its branches and a book she said her grandson loved. She is so kind that I give her a sudden hug that takes us both by surprise and she pats my head with a hand knotted by age and says I'm a good boy.

Christmas is quiet and brilliant. I give Mum a paper elephant because she loves elephants and a clock I made in DT. I didn't make the metal cogs by hand but I did fit them all together and I made the case out of clear plastic so she could see them all clicked together and turning. I think they're beautiful and I didn't want to hide them away. She says she loves it and she gives me a hug that holds the whole of me together. She gives me a Lego set so I can build and a glass ball that crackles and shoots out tendrils of lightning wherever you touch it and hundreds and hundreds of plain and patterned paper squares to fold. We eat too much and we watch a Christmas film that's so silly and funny that I laugh until my belly hurts and I forget everything except us.

That night I only make one paper shape before I fall asleep with just one little light burning.

ZOFIA

On New Year's Day Dad and I go to the beach to do the Dunk. The Dunk is legendary around here and it's maybe my favourite thing in the world. Everyone goes. All of Ceto Class are there with their families and we high-five and I wrestle Leo to the ground when he doesn't expect it and that means I'm winning 5–3.

We put on our wetsuits that stick and suck at our skin and Dad puts on goggles. I don't need them because I can open my eyes under the sea but Dad says it makes his eyeballs itch. A couple of people are tying flags to their waists and I feel a little lurch but it's OK. I've still got lots of time and it's too cold today.

The sea is bright and beautiful. It is ironclad like the sky but the greys twist together in rolls of silk. When I dive in it takes my breath away and I flip on to my back and stare up at the clouds.

The shouts and screams and shrieks bounce off the cliffs and then the sea is full of heads and legs and shards of flippers and flashes of goggle glass. We swim together and some people get out after five seconds and sit on the sand with flasks of coffee and some people swim to Fiji and tie their flags to the waiting poles and some people like me and Dad tread water and dive down and race each other. My body remembers exactly what to do and I'm part of the rolling waves again when I'm with Dad and it's just us and it's perfect.

TOM

When she tells me I think I must have misheard. That I've reshaped the words into my worst nightmare.

But she says them again.

I listen carefully. I don't want to drop a single syllable.

But it's the same the second time around.

I'd like us to move in with Marek and Zofia.

I don't scream or shout because I never scream or shout. I know not to make too much noise. Just in case. I let the words sink into my skin and into my bones and I grow cold. The panic that always crawls in my blood starts to twist and bite. I don't want to live with that girl and her father all those many miles away by the sea. I don't want to leave this little flat and leave my perfect little bedroom and leave my quiet school where nobody bothers me. I don't want to leave Mrs Adams and I don't want to start again all over again. I don't want to have to worry about what someone else is doing in my own house again. I don't want to. I don't want to. I don't want to. I say it in my head over and over and over and I hope that she hears.

But when I look up she's pink-cheeked and it's that same look she's carried for a while now. Happiness.

So I swallow down the words before they bubble up and I nod and I say *OK*. And I fold up that bit of paper that wants me to be happy and I let it crumble to ash.

ZOFIA

There's a reason that this is so quick. A reason that there's a whirlwind rush towards the worst possible thing in the world. A reason we all have to squash and squeeze together in my little cottage with my dad.

Fiona is having a baby.

I am more than a storm and I am more than a hurricane and I am more than a tempest. I am all fury balled up into one girl and I have lightning in me. It bites at my bones and burns in my blood.

As soon as those words have cracked the ground between us I run out of the door and Pablo chases my heels because it's all just a game for him. I run to the sea and I don't even have to remember to take off my shoes because I'm not wearing any and the stones and sand prick my feet. I dive under the dark water and I feel the stream of bubbles cascade from my nose and mouth and the icy knives of the waves but I don't really feel them. I don't feel the scratchsharp rawness of my torn toes or the saltsting of the water as it rushes at them. I swim and swim against the winter waves until I don't feel a single thing at all.

TOM

Mum is putting things in boxes. All our lives into brown cardboard again. The first time we packed there wasn't time for boxes and tape and removal vans. The second time we had black bin bags and twenty minutes and racing hearts.

Now she is wrapping things carefully in paper and examining cups and plates and pictures. *Shall we keep this do you think, or send it to charity? You know I've never liked this jug! Your great-aunt Margaret gave it to me but I think we can part ways now, I mean she died six years ago. Oh what about this vase? You know, Jo would probably love this. I'll give it to her at work tomorrow, a leaving present!*

I help her choose. This all feels like it's whirling and rushing and happening so fast that I'm spinning on my feet and the world is a blur around me. Even though we have longer now than we've ever had before. Even though the plan isn't secret and whispered and midnight. Even though it's been three months since the news that made everything wild and different. Mum has had time to finish her job and I've had time to finish spring term at school and we have time to pack so carefully. It still feels a rush and every day is measured by the whole new person growing inside her. My brother or sister.

It is still strange to see all of our life laid out. Everything is higgledy and patchwork. We've had to leave a lot behind and collect things as we go and now nothing quite goes together. But *we* went together and now it feels strange and scary because we're fitting in two and a half new people all at once and I'm not sure there's room.

I make a fort from the packing boxes. I want it to be three or four or maybe five storeys high and I want it to have six bedrooms and a swimming pool and a hockey field and a stable and battlements so tall they touch the skyceiling so I can peer down at intruders, which are only likely to be Dad or the cat or the dog but it's still good to have high ground. If I have the high ground I can shoot the arrows from my bow and they'll land right on target. No intruders allowed except maybe Pablo but he might eat the cardboard. He chewed through a cardboard dog-biscuit box and ate sixteen Bonios once and then he was very sick on the rug. I thought it was hilarious but Dad didn't think it was so funny because he had to clear it all up.

Anyway I make a fort from the boxes but I can only

make one storey with really really high walls because it turns out flattened cardboard box floors won't even take the weight of one average-sized cat. Frida hissed and ran away but she landed on her paws and she was the one who decided to test out the structural integrity so she can't really blame me, can she.

We have a thousand brown packing boxes but we're not actually moving. If we were moving I would be building my fort in the garden and Dad could go and live on his own. Maybe the new owners would adopt me. Maybe they wouldn't move in their pregnant girlfriend and her weird son. All my problems solved and a great opportunity to ask for more pocket money and maybe that pet tarantula. I'd call him Derek.

These boxes are for all the *junk*. Dad might call it junk but I think it's treasure. We might not use the rickety three-legged chairs or old lamps with ragged wires or rusty spanners or Mickey Mouse ears I got when I was five and the two of us went to Disneyland Paris but they're still our things and I think we should keep them. In fact, I put on the ears when I find them even though they pinch my head like an eagle's claw. I'm the Mouse King of the Castle. Good job Frida scarpered.

We're packing up two whole rooms. One is what Dad calls his *study* and also *the boxroom*, depending on how much work he's done that week. It's probably the right size for an actual mouse. When he's in there he looks like a human being that's been folded up all wrong. He is very tall, like he was made normal size and then someone stretched all his skin and skeleton up and up. His head grazes all the door frames and he stoops so often his spine traces the shape even when there's nothing above him. He calls me a titch even though I'm the tallest in Ceto Class including all the boys although Mo is catching up a bit.

The other room is the spare room which means it's for spare things, as far as I can tell. Spare things that are absolutely not junk. That's where I am building my fort even though technically I am meant to be putting things in the boxes and not creating a tiny empire. I poke a pile of stuff with my toe and it wobbles and shakes and for a moment I think that this is the way I'll die, crushed under every issue of the *British Medical Journal* from 1986 to the present.

I am preparing my final words but the pile rights itself again so I skulk round to the next one to see what I can find. Most of it is actually a bit junk-like but every so often I see something that I used to love, like my yellow plastic teapot or my collection of tin soldiers. I line them up around the perimeter of my fort and take the teapot inside. Crawling with a plastic teapot isn't easy and I'm just thinking that I should have made the door a bit higher when the actual door opens and Dad comes in. I am half in and half out of the fort, clutching a bright yellow teapot to my chest, wearing mouse ears intended for a five-year-old and surrounded by an army of tin soldiers. There is a large boxfort in the middle of the room. Other than that, things are pretty much as he left them.

Dad fills the air with his words and I imagine plucking apart the words with my hands and grinding them down like dust with my fingertips. First there are heavy grey granite words like ***disaster*** and ***furious*** and then there are ones that weigh a little bit less like *ridiculous* and *absurd* and then come ones that are light as air like *wild* and *feral*. Those are the words I like best. I know when he gets to feral that he's worked through the fury and swooped into laughter. And when he laughs it's OK to stop weighing words and imagining dusty language and scramble over to him and show him the bedrooms in my fort and where the swimming pool will go.

TOM

I say goodbye to Mrs Adams and I'm surprised because she cries. I feel funny when she does, so I fold a paper napkin into a flower and I give it to her. That makes her cry more and then she laughs and says she can't use it as a hanky now because it's too beautiful. I tell her I can make her more if she'd like and she says I'm a good boy and a brave boy. The second bit is her kindness again, because of all the many things I will never be, brave is top of the list. It's number one. It's circled and underlined. She holds the flower in her papery hands and she says *you know that the Japanese have a belief that if you make a thousand paper birds called cranes you get a wish, isn't that lovely?* And it is.

She gives me a blue bobble hat she's knitted for me and a yellow bobble hat she's knitted for the baby so we can sort of match and then she gives me a five-pound note from her purse. I try to say no to the money but she puts it into my hand and folds my fingers over it and says *look after your mum, Tom*.

I look at the yellow hat later. It is row after row of careful neat stitches in careful neat lines. It is impossibly small in my hands and I can't believe there will ever be a head tiny enough for it to fit. I feel a tug of something inside me and it flickers and leaps brighter and louder than the tendrils of panic that live in my bones. I put the hat in my box of paper shapes.

That night I learn the folds of paper cranes. I make seven long-necked sharp-winged birds and I put them in an empty cardboard packing box.

I start to imagine wishes. I start to imagine them coming true.

I am allowed to take a break from boxfort building, or *packing* as Dad would call it, to have some hot tea and toast. I make everything and I only drop one small splash of milk and two slices of bread. And that basically didn't happen because Pablo disappears them in seconds. When I bring the tray to the kitchen table Dad beams and tells me how helpful I am.

Dad drinks his tea black with sugar and lemon. I tried that once and it was completely disgusting. It was like someone had put the teabag directly into my throat and then thoughtfully added a whack of sourness that made my eyes stream. I didn't even notice the sugary warmth because I was too busy hacking and retching and being called feral. I drink my tea with milk instead like Mum did, but I do have the same type of cup as Dad. They're glass cups with metal handles that slot on so you don't burn your fingerprints off and they're what Polish people use for tea. British people use china mugs with splays of patterns, anything from kittens and flowers to swear words. I'm half and half so maybe I should write something rude on my glass cup with a Sharpie and then draw Frida on it. Dad always says you shouldn't drink from anything you can't see all the way through and then he mimes choking from poison which is pretty rich considering what happened when he made me try his tea. And anyway if someone was going to poison you, you'd think they'd go to the trouble of mixing it in so you couldn't see it.

Dad sips his tea and ignores another copy of the *British Medical Journal* that will probably later join the pile and be the thing that causes it to topple and squash the cat. Poor Frida hasn't even recovered from falling through the battlements yet. I feed Pablo pieces of toast and he licks off all the Marmite and then drops the bready bits on the floor because he's a very strange dog.

This table is going to feel a bit small soon says Dad

and I look up guiltily because feeding the dog from the table is just about number one on the list of things that the Happy Hound dog-training man said we shouldn't do after Pablo ate the TV remote and also most of the sofa. I make a noise that wheezes out like a pig grunt and Dad rolls his eyes and tries again. *Maybe we should get a bigger one?* I grunt again. I like our table. Mum and Dad made it from floorboards glued together when they didn't have any money and they didn't have me but they did have some floorboards. I wrote my name on it in careful pen strokes when I was four and I like seeing how the Z is backwards like a spiky S even though I'm forever having to say *no it's Zofia actually. With a Z. No, not Sofia. Yes, like Sofia. But with a* Z and so on and so on and for forever and then another day.

We could go to IKEA tomorrow he says and I perk up because IKEA has both meatballs and those little pencils that make me feel like a giant, but then he says *maybe Fiona and Tom will want to go too* and I try not to growl out loud. And then he remembers something else and rifles through the pages of his battered black diary and he's busy tomorrow anyway. I grunt for a third time and feed the last of my toast to Pablo. I leave the slimy remains on the floor for Dad to step in when he gets up. I don't feel like being helpful any more.

TOM

It's my last day at Treverton Primary.

This isn't like before. Mum keeps saying it. *It's not like before, Tom, this is a positive move and it's so much better for us. Think of the sea air! You can go swimming* and then her voice fades into soft silence because she remembers and she knows I won't want to go swimming where there are rip tides and

Currents. Jellyfish. Sharks and

Seaweed that wraps itself around your legs and pulls you down and

Salt water that burns your eyes and your skin and your lungs when you try to breathe but there's no sky left.

At school everyone has signed a card for me, even George who called me a chickenboy and squawked last week when I wouldn't jump off the gym horse and Mr Mackie had to help me down. No one has written anything except their names and a few *see you soon*s which isn't true. It's just what you write when you don't know what else to say. No one really minds that I'm leaving because I don't say much in class or play much at playtime and I've only been here since Year 5 and they've all known each other since infants. I am the weird one. I once asked Connor if he knew how to make light into a rainbow and paper back into a tree and he told everyone I was deranged. After that no one really wanted to talk to me any more.

I sit quietly on the edges and there will be no empty space left when I go.

When the final bell goes I get my coat and my bag and I walk out into the watery spring sunshine without looking back.

I don't think I mind very much.

I'm used to moving around.

This time will be different though. Like Mum says.

It won't just be us any more.

I go to the beach without Dommo because I clearly need to get some more practice in. I pull on my wetsuit and scrabble around at the back for the long ribbon attached to the zip. I practically have to turn myself inside out to reach it and pull it all the way to the top. Once I'm sealed up I wade into the waves. Pablo barks behind me but he doesn't come any further because even though he's quite stupid he's not *that* stupid. The sea is freezing and the flesh on my wrists is turning an interesting shade of purple. I look down at my water-washed feet and they're ghoulish green in the sealight. I close my eyes and rush forward and crash under the surface with a splash like a gunshot.

But instead of the whole world changing, and everything becoming quiet and faraway and perfect, something is wrong. Again. This isn't like the Dunk and this isn't like the bathtub and this isn't like all those first rolling salt-bloomed swims that made me feel brand new and brilliant.

Instead of a green-tinged rippled underworld I keep seeing Dad and Fiona and Tom all together with a new baby. They're laughing and Dad ruffles Tom's hair. I'm not in the picture. That feeling of being fresh and new and faraway is fading and instead it's jellyfish-sting skin and lungs made of rock. I draw in air like it's coming through a straw. I kick and turn and weave through the water and I keep doing it until my muscles are screaming and I keep doing it until the screaming is so loud I can't ignore it any more. My heart is trying to escape my ribcage. My eyes dot with stars and black jellyfish shapes that seem to leap across the sky. Something is happening to me and I can't stop it and I flip on to my back and count the clouds and try to breathe. After I get to twenty clouds my heart has stopped its bid for freedom and my lungs aren't frozen stiff.

I tread water and stare at Fiji. Can it move? Does it move? It seems further away than ever even though the shore is far behind me. I want to keep swimming towards it but I'm not stupid because I know if I get even more tired and I'm still on my way out to sea then I'll probably drown. So I make my way slowly slowly back to the shore and back to Pablo who has found a seagull to make friends with. I'm not sure the seagull is overly keen.

I drip my way back up the path to the house and I shake myself off like a dog in the front garden so Dad can't complain too much about the floor inside getting wet. Then I have a bath so hot it steams up all the windows and turns me pink from my toes to the top of my head.

Afterwards I go to our spare room. It's empty now except for a new single bed that was delivered yesterday. The big window that faces the sea is ajar so that the outside wind can sweep away the stale air. The room is filled with a salt tang and the smell of seaweed. I don't understand what just happened to me. I'm a good swimmer. I sit in the middle of the floor in my dressing gown and Frida climbs on to my lap.

TOM

The flat is empty. You can see the dark outlines of where our furniture was pressed up against the white walls. A ghost sofa and a ghoulish gallery of pictures. Everything was either given away or sold online or loaded up into a big van this morning by a huge man called Nev and his two silent sons.

All my special things were the last things to be boxed up. Mum wanted everything to be packed away the night before we go so Nev could be quick when he arrived, but I couldn't have a whole night without them. I fold paper cranes until the morning light starts to creep its fingers through my curtains.

I packed up all my things myself. Some of the things don't look very important but they are to me. The paper city. Flaps of birds and bright-nosed foxes folded from squares. Bits of wood I've glued into the shape of a tiny birdhouse. A very old watch with cogs that look like they're all in a jumble inside but they're all in exactly the right place and they all work together perfectly. Or nearly. I need to learn how to make it tick.

I put my torch in my pocket.

Mum is hoovering even though I'm not sure she should be because of the baby. She says it's fine but I take over anyway and the *hmmm* and *grr* of the vacuum cleaner fills my head. I push it over and over the greying carpets until the bag is bursting with dust. I empty it and wash my hands and look around. This is the last time it will be just us. I've never packed slowly before. I've never left a flat empty.

Last time I didn't even get to take my torch.

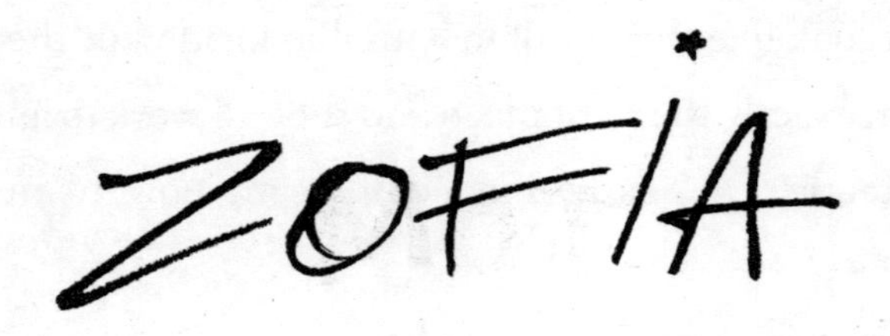

It's our last evening just the two of us. I can't really believe that's true and I keep thinking what if they decide not to come or what if it's all been a terrible dream because I ate loads of cheese before bed. But my love of dairy is mostly restricted to milkshakes and Oreos, and when I pinch myself it really hurts.

Dad makes me beans on toast with extra hot sauce just the way I like it and then he lets me have a milkshake even though they're meant to be for weekends only. We curl up on the sofa and watch my favourite Ghibli film and he doesn't say anything at all about how weird he thinks they are and I feel a plunge of something sharp in my tummy and it's not the chilli sauce. We're not going to have an evening like this ever again.

TOM

The next day we drive down in Mum's old blue car. It rattles when it goes too fast and I grip the sides of my seat until my knuckles pop. I'm glad we're not in the big van with Nev though. I saw his knuckles when he gripped our boxes and they were huge and angry.

I said goodbye to the flat before we left and I got to walk from room to empty room and there was no whisper-quiet panicky rush and one bag each and tiptoes and leaving when the moon is full.

We swing through lanes that get greener and bloom with life. The world is turning wild and the city feels small and far away. I feel small and far away.

My box of special things is on the back seat and it's strapped in. I wouldn't let Nev take it. He rolled his eyes like Dad and went back to his van with a box of plates instead. I could feel his irritation and though he didn't say a word I could still see it clouded and fogged around us in a furious swirl.

Mum said my special box would be fine in the van but what if Nev brakes too fast or streaks around a corner or crashes off a cliff?

We go to the beach after school and I want to stay forever but everyone has plans and after about half an hour the light fades and so does Ceto Class. Dommo and I stay and we sit and share her Oreos and we throw a ball for Pablo for a bit and try to stretch out the afternoon into evening and maybe into night but then Dommo looks at her diving watch and says we need to get back. I shout *no let's go for a swim* and I run to the edge of the water and I rush in wearing my shoes and Pablo chases after me and gets cold paws and he barks in alarm and Dommo throws her arms up and shouts back that I'm a loon but she runs down to the waves too and we paddle and sing stupid songs at the sky for just a little while longer.

Dommo sees it before I do because I'm trying to persuade Pablo not to eat gravel. She stops by her front door and calls *today already? You didn't say anything* and I look up and I see her looking at the big truck parked in my front garden. I stand up straight too quickly and blood rushes and stars prick and dance in front of the massive chunk of white metal that's here to ruin my life.

I stomp into the kitchen even though I can't quite manage a stomp because my shoes are full of seawater. I squelch into the kitchen and stop short. It's empty. I look up at the big clock on the wall that ticks off all the too-quick seconds before school starts in the morning and the too-slow minutes when Dad is late home from work. But it's definitely time and I was barely even late and the van is right there outside.

But there's nothing but silence. I don't like silence.

I squelch upstairs and shout as I go so Dad will poke his face out of his study, except I'd forgotten that it's not his study any more. But he does poke his face out and it's splattered with something yellow. I think for a moment that maybe he's caught something horrible from one of his patients in the hospital. But as I get closer I can see it's not just Dad who is yellow. He's painted the whole little room a bright bouncing sunbeam yellow. He's grinning like he invented the colour himself.

Brilliant, isn't it! So cheerful!

I nod slowly because I think I might actually be losing the sight in both eyes. It's very very very bright.

I think the baby will love it says Dad happily and just like that all of the colour drains out of everything.

TOM

When we pull up outside the house Nev has already arrived and he's waiting impatiently in his van with his sons. He huffs and puffs about people not knowing the quickest way anywhere any more and the swirling cloud around him darkens with his words but Mum smiles and thanks him for waiting and the cloud blows away on the wind.

I let my breath out too.

Nev and his sons open the van doors and as they do the door of the cottage opens. Marek is standing there with his arms spread out wide.

He pulls Mum into them and for a moment it's just the two of them illuminated against the porch.

Marek reaches out to ruffle my hair and I snap my head back so fast I can feel the wind whistle around my ears. The air hangs empty between us and I can feel panic tingling.

He puts his hands in his pockets and says *it's so good to have you here, Tom, I've been looking forward to this day for a long time. Would you like to see your room?* His words are soft but I still look at Mum and she's nodding and saying she'll be up in a minute because she needs to show Nev where to put our stuff, but I don't go with Marek. I wait until Mum is finished pointing out the right spaces to Nev and then we go together.

ZOFIA

There's a feather-soft knock on my door and Dad says *Zofia, will you come and say hello* but I won't. I won't come out of here until they've realised this is all a terrible mistake and it's just me and Dad and Frida and Pablo again.

Or until I'm really really hungry.

TOM

Mum and Marek show me my bedroom together. It has pale grey walls that slope and slide because this cottage is very old. The seawinds have breathed it into its shape. The room has a wooden floor and I can see straightaway that there are gaps between the boards where dark can hide.

It has a large window that faces the sea. Marek thinks that's great and he keeps pointing it out but I don't want to look and it makes me feel giddy when I do. The way the waves rock backwards and forwards and roll against the sky is like being on a ship. At first it makes me feel seasick on land but I can't quite look away. Sunlight blooms on the water.

Marek points upwards to the ceiling and Mum squeezes my arm so I look too and there are a thousand plastic stars glued in swirls and galaxies. They have a milky green glow even in daylight and I know they'll be brighter when night creeps in. Marek smiles and says he put them up today because he thought I'd like them.

I do like them and I don't know what to say because it is a kind thing to do. But I also know that kindness can change.

Dad built me a train track that looped all the way round the living room once.

ZOFIA

Obviously I am really really hungry about an hour after they arrive. Lunch was a very long time ago and Oreos might be delicious but they're not very filling. My tummy growls and Frida looks alarmed. The van skids off and spits gravel at the windows and Pablo barks and I am still in my room. No one has even come to get me or see if I'm all right or offer me any snacks or check if I'm dead from starvation.

I stomp downstairs in my salt-stiff socks and stand in the doorway to the kitchen. The three of them are sitting at my backwards Z Zofia table eating plates of steaming pasta. Pablo has his head on that boy's knee. Traitor. He's only in it for the spaghetti. Dad turns and says *there you are, kochanie, come and have something to eat* but there's basically not any room with Tom and Fiona there. Fiona has one hand on Tom's hand and the other on her stomach like she's already soothing the baby.

The stupid baby. It ruined everything and it's not even born yet and it won't be for months. One minute it's all let's-live-apart then it's let-Tom-finish-his-school-term-and-Fiona-finish-her-job-contract-in-the-city and then suddenly it's quick quick come and invade our home as soon as you possibly can, *please*! It still took ages to organise because of boring things like jobs and schools and I kept thinking it might not happen and they'd stay in the faraway city and I'd maybe see them once every few weeks like I was forced to do until now and the only thing that would be different from that would be a screeching baby in the corner. But then the date was in the diary and then it was on the horizon and finally it was crashing down like a wave.

They all look so perfect sitting there. Father and mother and baby on the way and little boy and dog all bathed in the seaglow light. It's like something from an advert where they're really trying to sell you chicken stock but instead they're selling you this warm hug of family. Tom feeds Pablo a bit of spaghetti. I wait for Dad to tell Tom off like he does when I do it but instead he just laughs and my blood fizzes. Tom giggles and says in surprise *his tongue tickles.* Dad has already forgotten about me standing in the doorway waiting for some space to be made for me. I look at them laughing together and getting the dog to exchange an outstretched paw for an ear scratch and a piece of pasta and I don't want spaghetti any more.

I slip back down to the beach and stare at the roll of the waves. The moon is bright tonight and I am alone except for the sounds of the sea.

TOM

The first night I don't sleep.

I have all of my lights and my torch and my own duvet and my origami paper and my box of carefully packed special things.

I try to count the stars above me and I try to empty all of the thoughts from my brain like they're grains of salt in a shaker. Every time I start to sink into sleep the slap and crash of the waves startles me back to the surface. I stare at the star-splashed ceiling instead. I fold paper into stars but they keep crumpling under my hands and even folding won't stop the trembling tonight. I make paper crane after paper crane because it feels more important than ever but they're crooked and bent. Their necks lean sadly to one side and their wings are crumpled and broken.

I want to be happy for Mum. I want to be good and

be kind and be brave and I don't want to make a fuss. I don't want Mum to know that I just want it to be me and her and that I don't want to be here. Mum told me Zofia is afraid of not having Marek all to herself any more and I wanted to shout me too. But then I don't think Zofia has been afraid of anything in her whole life. She just doesn't want me here.

I thought I might be nervous of living with Pablo because he's quite big and bouncy and when I first met him he jumped up and I fell backwards. But I like him a lot. Marek told me he's a labradoodle and that means he's half idiot and half tornado. Marek also said he's been having some lessons in how to be more polite and I liked it when he ate spaghetti from my hand at supper and he was so gentle and he looked at me for more.

In the morning when I get up, but don't wake up because I never found sleep, I have a new uniform again. It is actually just a green jumper and whatever trousers and shoes you like. You can take slippers to school to wear inside, which is strange but Mum says it'll be fun and we just need to buy some slippers for me.

Zofia is sitting at the kitchen table which has her name written on it and she's scowling and kicking her feet. Pablo is waiting for her to drop some toast for him but when he sees me he gets up and scrambles over to say hello. I scratch his ears and Zofia's scowl darkens and when I sit down she gets up. I feel a tiny spike of something and I'm pleased she's gone and I'm pleased Pablo came to me.

I have to walk the dog-stealing boy to school. He doesn't look very happy when Dad tells us but he doesn't say anything and he goes and brushes his teeth and washes his face without even being asked like the goody two shoes he is. Dad says *you have to be kind and you have to be brave, Zofia. I know this is different and difficult for you, darling* and I hiss like Frida and stop listening because I am always brave and I'm not afraid and I don't find things difficult, so what is he talking about?

We tramp along the gravel. Dommo comes out of her house and says in a voice that's meant to be a whisper *is that him then* and the tips of Tom's ears turn pink like the very edges of scallop shells. He says *hello* in a little pipsqueak voice and Dommo walks next to him and starts talking about something on Cartoon Network at rapid speed. Tom blinks and nods along.

We walk down the beach path that is surrounded by dark plum heather and whiskery tufts of seagrass. The sea is turning blue in the morning air and I wander closer to the shore but Tom stays on the path with Dommo and looks straight ahead.

Does anyone want to swim before school I shout across the sand and I surprise myself. I don't really want to share my ocean with him but the lap of the waves and the smell of the sea is drawing me towards it like a magnet. Dommo looks interested and turns to Tom but he shakes his head no in a birdwing head-flutter of panic and I feel steam boiling in my blood again and I stamp back towards them.

I don't really like water he whispers, but to Dommo and not me and I think you baby you baby you baby. Dommo says *we'd be late if we did anyway, Tom, and it's really cold this morning to be fair* and I throw her a look that could crack the sky and we walk the rest of the way in a silence that growls between us.

TOM

I could never say yes to the swim. The sea wasn't bright and glittering like it was in the dark last night. It had changed completely and I liked it even less. It was cold and a steel grey that covered deep dark depths.

Dad would have made me get in. When we went to the seaside he grabbed my hand and he pulled me into the water and he shouted that we were having a brilliant time and I wasn't having a brilliant time at all because I am pathetic and I couldn't be brave then or now. The water dragged me down and streamed up my nose and at the last second he pulled me up and while stars were bursting in my eyes and salt scraping my lungs he said *you didn't really think I'd let you drown, did you?*

And all those memories bubbled their way into my brain and I said no and Dommo was nice and Zofia didn't say another word.

In the playground before morning bell everyone is crowded around the hopscotch squares watching Jacob and Jude attempt to get from one end to the other with their legs tied together. Dommo says *Tom, come and meet everyone* and I can't believe her because she knows what I think about Tom.

Ceto Class shout over to us and it's a tangle of voices and tied-together legs and *all right, Dommo, all right, Zofia* and *who's this* and then everyone is very interested in Tom, and Leo says *our class has six boys now we're winning we're winning* and I give him a small kick in the shins which makes him yelp.

Tom looks like he's been pulled from another universe. The last new person in our class was Alma and that was three years ago and so everyone is all keen and interested and it's like they can't see what's flashing neon in front of them.

He's ruined my life and I was here first.

These are my friends and this is my school and it's my house and my dad and my dog and my life.

TOM

There are only ten other pupils in my new class. It's a lot quieter than my old school even with Zofia around. Although she's been almost silent since we got into the playground. It's a bit odd to see her but not hear her. Even her walk is usually loud and her arms windmill and catch the air. She's a tornado of sounds and movement and energy. She says so many words and expresses so many things that the air is a riot of noise and whirling limbs. Now it's like somebody has pressed pause and she's stuck and silent. I can feel the anger coming off her in shoots and sparks even if her face stays exactly the same and even if she doesn't say a word. I can feel something else and I think it's hurt and sadness. I want to say something. The anger that simmers inside is melting slowly. She looks lost.

I want to ask her if she's OK and that this is strange for me too. I want to say it's not my fault. I want to say I'm sorry anyway. I want to say I'm unhappy. I want to say I'm sad. But the bell rings and we are swept inside on the tide of children.

I sit next to a boy called Cameron and he shows me where to hang my jacket and where to put my shoes for when I have my own slippers. Cameron's have monkey faces and I like them a lot. The teacher Miss Cassidy doesn't make a big fuss about me being new and me living with Zofia and being her nearly stepbrother. She just smiles and says in a soft voice that she'll be in the classroom at morning break if I want to ask her anything. It all feels simple and easy and for a moment some of the swirling fireworks of panic that have been blasting from my brain and into every nerve since forever ago stop.

I am sent to the nurse's office during morning class because I have been so quiet that Miss Cassidy decides I must be ill. I sit in the little room that smells of plasters and old sick and listen to a reception child cough himself silly. I am quite close to seeing if he'd feel better if I put him in the bin when the nurse comes in and feels my forehead and asks if I'm feeling poorly. I shake my head ferociously because I'm never unwell but she looks at me and says *you're not yourself, I can still hear myself think* and so she rings home.

Dad is at work and I know Fiona had some scan this morning so I'm hoping she's not around to come and get me. I'm worried she might try to show me a picture of the baby or ask what I think about the name Grizelda or something.

But she answers the phone, so she's back and she's

the one who has to pick me up. I think she can probably see the stormcloud gathering above my head. She looks at me with concern all over her face and I notice her eyes are a bit pink around the rims. Like a mouse. She says *I brought the car in case you couldn't manage the walk* and I roll my eyes because it takes approximately four minutes to get from the school to back home and unless the nurse told her both my legs had been involved in an unfortunate shark-biting incident then why on earth wouldn't I be able to *manage* that.

I get into her ancient blue car that smells like petrol and rubber and she fastens her seatbelt around the small roundness of her belly. I don't think I could see a bump yesterday. But babies grow all the time, don't they. It'll probably only fit in the boxroom for about a week and then it'll be given my room and I'll have to sleep on the beach. Which I would actually love but that's not really the point.

Fiona fumbles with the key in the ignition. Her hand has a white plaster on the back of it like she's had an injection. She probably has. They do all sorts to you when you're having a baby. The car coughs. It sounds like it's quite close to death and the engine rattles. I'm not sure it will manage the journey home any better than I would with two legs bitten off by sharks.

You OK, love she says and I glare at her because I am no one's love. She holds her hands up as if I'm aiming my bow and arrow at her which in my head I am and then starts to drive off.

Was Tom all right she asks and I can see she's really worried and I know Dad said that Tom has been to a lot of schools and I start to wonder if maybe he's actually a tiny wildchild who's been expelled from every school from here to Timbuktu and she's checking if he's kicked off and set fire to the gym yet. She sniffs like she has a cold.

Fine I say. It's a short word and I somehow make it even shorter. What I don't say is that everyone seems to love him and he and Cameron were giggling into their fractions at the back during maths (giggling! At fractions!) and that he'd swept in and stolen my Ceto Class from right under my nose just like he stole my dog and my dad and my spare room.

I shrug and she sighs and grips the steering wheel

as we pull out of the school car park. I roll down the window a bit to smell the sea and not the inside of her car. *It's just he's such a nervous boy and he's so quiet and he's been through a lot and I worry a bit, you know, you know what mums are like* and then she stops the words that are cascading out of her mouth and she looks horrified because of course I don't have a mother any more because she went and died. People always look like that when they think they've put their foot in it. I haven't had a mother since I was a tiny baby and my memories of her are all from old photographs and videos that are like someone else's life. She's a story that sometimes I like to be told but you can't miss what you can't remember. But I do quite enjoy how uncomfortable she looks so I turn my face to the window as if my feelings are bruised.

We pull on to the gravel and Pablo goes absolutely wild when I walk in the door. He's a blur of curly fur and clattering paws and I want to go straight down to the beach with him but I'm meant to be ill so I go upstairs. Fiona tells me she'll make me something to eat in a bit and for now she's going to make some phone calls but to please please call her if I need anything at all. I ignore her completely.

I am about to go into my room and lie on the bed and maybe read a book or maybe plot how to get back at Tom for being a stealing life-stealer when I see his bedroom door is ajar. No not his bedroom. Our spare room. Mine and Dad's.

I go in because why shouldn't I. It belongs to me. I can hear Fiona's voice on the phone. Her voice is low so I can't catch the words but she doesn't sound happy. Maybe she's already so unhappy she'll leave and take that boy with her.

The window in the spare room is open and there is a saltwater tang to the air that's as familiar as my own skin but other than that it's completely different. Everything is in a new place and it's all different. A different bed and a new chest of drawers and a rug patterned with cars (he really must be five, honestly) and a ceiling speckled with plastic stars.

There are sheets and sheets of square paper in a thousand different colours arranged neatly on top of his desk. All of their edges line up perfectly and I fight the urge to ruffle them all up. Some of the squares have been folded into shapes. I can see an angular paper dog and a box and a boat and what I think is a skyscraper. I reach out a finger and thumb and I squash the box flat and then I panic and drop it behind his chest of drawers.

There's a big box with a lid underneath his desk and I flip it open and it's full of a rainbow of strange paper shapes that look like they could be broken-necked birds or maybe dinosaurs or maybe they're those dinosaurs that can fly. There are so many of them that they flap around the edges of the box and I roughly put the lid back on to keep them trapped. It won't go on properly because it's catching on something and I pull a scrap of yellow wool free and hold it up. It's a tiny hat for a tiny head, knitted in wavy sea lines. I feel a hot burn of something in my chest and I throw the hat on the floor in a sad ball.

Tom has lots of lights. A lava lamp blobs lazily in the corner and there's an alarm clock that glows different colours and a strange bulb pointing straight at pieces of glass that look like diamonds and somehow make rainbows on the wall and at least another four lamps dotted on top of unpacked boxes. Some of them would throw light up to the ceiling and some of them would fling it sideways and some of them would point it down at the ground. I'd bet that at night with the curtains closed and these bulbs all blazing there's not a single whisper of darkness in this room. Is he some sort of weird light-collector? Does he go round charity shops and little antique shops and funny dusty markets to try and find as many different lamps as he can? Does he store light in his pockets ready for any occasion?

He's even weirder than I thought. I lie on my bed later and eat the biscuits Fiona brought me and ignore the banana she's sliced into bite-sized pieces because I don't like fruit and she doesn't know me at all. I close my eyes and think about how everything was better before.

TOM

When the last bell of the day trings something strange happens. No one rushes off to waiting parents or to screeching buses clouding the streets with grey exhaust. No one forms little groups that are so tight around the edges that it's impossible to squeeze in. Instead everyone in the whole class starts walking together. And I walk with them. Dommo says it's a shame that Zofia isn't well because she's the absolute best at volleyball but it does mean the teams will be even and I realise she's asking me to play. I've never played volleyball before. I've played football at my old schools and with Dad in the garden. I hated every second and my legs never felt like they belonged to my body. Dad would throw his arms up and shout and tell me I was as useless as a girl. That didn't make sense because Zoe Hunter was the best at football at Treverton Primary but you didn't argue with Dad.

My mouth is dry and my heart sticks to my ribs. I don't want this new class to know how useless I am. I don't want there to be another Incident. I don't want them to laugh at me when my arms and legs twitch and skid and spin in the wrong directions and the ball thumps on the sand beside me. Everyone here seems to wear a different skin to me. They are toughened by the salt and the sea and the sun and the sand. I am milkpale and raw and my muscles are only used for trembling.

The beach is beautiful. I didn't look at it properly this morning. I just saw grey then. The sea has left its fingerprints on the sand so that it's patterned with golden waves. The sea matches the sky. They are both cloaked in emerald and they share the spring-bleached sunlight. But the sound of the sea slapping against the rocks and the knifeteeth of the cliffs that climb into the clouds makes me shudder and when Dommo dives into the water I wait breathless until her head breaks the surface again. No one else swims because it's just not warm enough and I'm glad I don't have to make excuses.

Leo and Mo set up the volleyball game and Cameron and I sit together and do our maths homework. His book is salt-stained and soon my pages are scratchy with sand. It's strange to sit in the cold at what feels like the very edge of the whole world and do fractions.

The volleyball game is not what I thought it would be because no one really seems to care about winning. Or keeping score. Or keeping the ball in the air. The first time the ball sails towards me I feel fear pricking the inside of my skin and fizzing to the ends of my nerves and I slap the ball down. It hits the ground with a thunk and sand spits. I wait for the shouts and groans and *you idiot*s and *what's wrong with you*s but they don't happen. Halima picks up the ball and punches it back over the raggedy net and Jude dives head first into a tangle of seagrass. The ball rolls gently to a rest just in front of his nose and Jacob picks it up. And we go again. We are the worst two volleyball teams in existence and I start to forget the slap of the sea and the looming cliffs and the sun quietly slipping down towards the horizon and I start to have fun.

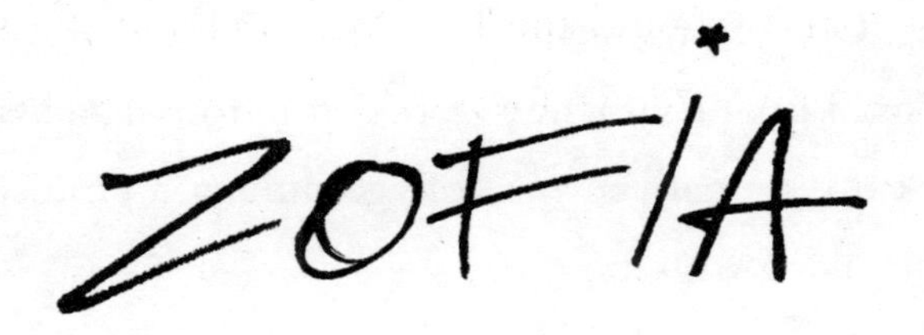

I stand on the edge of the beach, holding the leather loop of Pablo's lead. He is straining at the other end, desperate to pull towards his friends and the ball and the sea and the sounds. But I stay still as a statue.

Tom is splayed on the sand, the volleyball beside him. Dommo is laughing so hysterically that the noise bounces off the cliffs and fills the sky. The laughter grows to a chorus like the screech of circling gulls as the rest of Class 6 joins in. As Tom joins in. I have barely heard him talk before now and suddenly there's this rich deep giggle that is too big to come from something so small. He looks completely different. His whole face has broken open and the pale pinched boy is gone. He is pink-cheeked and the stiffness in his bones that spread its way all through his body has evaporated. He looks like one of them. One of the gang. One of my gang.

And I can't bear it any more. I spin round and walk back up the path to the cottage pulling a protesting Pablo along with me.

I get home and I don't say a word. I go upstairs to the bathroom and run the water until it splashes the floorboards and I don't care. I sink beneath the surface and I wait for the feeling of calm and the song of the water to take me somewhere else but it doesn't. I can't stay under. I can't let my lungs stay still and grow strong. The seconds stretch for hours and

One

Two

Three four

fivesixseven

I burst the water like a bubble and breathe until the stars in my eyes fade to nothing.

TOM

Zofia is still ill and she's in the bathroom when I get back from school and the beach. Mum and Marek are talking in low voices in the kitchen but they stop when I come in. Mum says Zofia had felt a bit better and even took the dog out but then felt ill all over again and had to come back. I know it's mean but I'm glad. Even if I felt sorry for her earlier things are easier when she's not around. Mum takes her some soup and bread in her room and when she comes back she looks sad and I know Zofia has been mean and my heart pinches.

I have supper with Marek and Mum and we talk about the beach and school and new jobs and we're laughing together and it feels nice even if I don't trust Marek yet. Mum has a scan picture to show me. It's grainy and strange and the baby glows against the black of Mum's insides. It is folded up like one of my paper creations and at first it looks more like a shrimpy alien than a baby. But as I stare the blurry shapes start to fit together and I see the tracing of a nose and a mouth and a tiny hand stretching out to say hello. I feel another little tug of something inside me.

We talk about names for the baby. Mum and Marek don't know if it's a boy or a girl and Mum says she doesn't mind and she doesn't want to find out and she says it doesn't matter and other things are more important but she doesn't say what. Marek squeezes her hand. I'm not sure I want it to be a girl if it means it will be like Zofia. Marek suggests a load of stupid name choices like Vanderbeek and Rolltop and Xanadu and Bathtap and Mum hits him with her napkin and just like that all the salted softness that melted into my bones on the beach and when I saw the baby waving is gone. I flinch. Mum sees straight-away and she reaches out her gentle hands to me and I take one but my heart is a thunderclap.

When I go upstairs I know something is wrong. My careful paper city is askew. The lids on the boxes under my desk have been lifted off and put back the wrong way. When I open the boxes I can see crushed shapes and broken paper wings. The secret little yellow hat is scrunched in a ball on the floor.

She has been in my room. *She* has looked at my things. A mixture of old and new feelings starts to swirl and swim inside me and I can't push them down and fold them up and put them away. They bubble under my skin until they burst through and swirl around me.

I wake up in the morning with eyes sticky from sleep and I yawn and stretch out as wide as I can and accidentally shove the cat off the bed. She growls and huffs over to the door and shouts to be let out. I can't even keep the cat on my side. I stroke her head and she gives a reluctant purr and I am being nice and kind and gentle and it's working so perhaps I should give that a go downstairs.

I tell Dad that I am definitely better and definitely well enough for school. He sees people who are about four million per cent sicker than me every day at the hospital so the fact that I was standing upright and speaking was enough to convince him to let me go to school. He wasn't paying much attention anyway. His face was already clouded with thoughts about all the patients he had to see today and all the things he needed to do and all the places he needed to be and all the people he needed to be there for. He gives me a kiss on top of my head and says *please be good today, Zofia, it's so important* and then he fades into the morning mist outside.

I try to be extra nice because I want Dad to know I'm his best one. I help Fiona put out the breakfast things, and I clear them all away without even being asked and she beams at me like I've bought her a puppy but she's not even really looking at me either. It's like I've faded pale and ghostly. I wash my face and brush my teeth. I bare them in the mirror and snap them together like a wolf and I'm definitely not invisible. Snowdrops of toothpaste speckle the mirror and I even try to wipe them off but I make things a bit worse. I tried though.

I am extra specially nice to Tom. I smile at him and I keep my wolfteeth hidden. I talk about school and the summer and football and the beaches and he doesn't say a word and when I look right at him he's got something on his knee and he makes a little frog-noise and he hasn't been listening to a word

I've said. I thump my fist on the table to show I'm flesh and blood and bone and I'm not a ghostly girl fading to nothing. He jumps and the air around him trembles.

I tried I TRIED I TRIED I want to scream but for once my voice won't come out right.

I heard them last night all laughing at the table and making stupid jokes. I clatter some more plates into the sink and as I do it I see something on the fridge. It's a black picture with a ghost in the middle. I step towards it and I see the shape of a baby floating in the gloom. Their baby. I feel sick.

I am squashed and squeezed out of my own house and my own family and everything is unravelling like the edges of a scarf. I am unravelling, my wool unspooling and I don't feel part of anything or whole or enough any more. I want Tom to go away. I want Fiona to go away. I want the baby to go away. I wish the baby would disappear.

I run down to the beach. I stand in the biting morning saltwind and I feel the tide ebb and flow in time with my raging hurt. I am a storm and I am the sea and when we are one I hurl my wish on the water and I wish upon the waves just like in Dad's story and I cross my fingers so tightly and I wish I wish I wish.

TOM

I managed seven seconds last night before I flicked on every light and made the dark scuttle back into the cracks. The dark is different here. There is nothing but black air. No trickle of street lamps or headlights or the buzz of neon signs. It is everything. It feels like it might swallow me whole.

Zofia is so loud in the morning that her voice is starting to make my teeth shake and my head pound. I want to shout back at her and I want to tell her I know she's been through my things but I'm not brave enough.

She is so loud. I can't put my hands over my ears because that's rude so I curl in a corner and eat my toast as quickly as I can. While I'm eating I use one hand to fold an old receipt into a frog. I try to concentrate on each line and fold and corner and fill my head with something that isn't the noise of her. I hop the frog on my knee and I make a tiny ribbit noise before I can stop myself and Zofia stops whatever she's yelling about and her hand makes a fist. It thumps and shakes the table. I jump before I can stop my bones from twitching and she looks right at me. There's hot fury in her eyes and I wonder what she sees in mine.

After I've wished what I wished I am even louder than usual. I know I am. I can feel my bounce and my shouts vibrating in the wind. Dommo once claimed I'd made her lose her hearing for three days after we went on a school trip to a medieval castle and even she looks surprised by how loud I'm being. I can't seem to turn myself down. I'm trying to make as much noise as possible to shut up an awful gnawing inside me. Dad jokes that my volume button is broken but it really feels like it today. I feel broken. As we walk along the path and into the playground I get louder and louder and louder until the concrete beneath my feet feels like it's cracking. I flit from person to person telling jokes and turning cartwheels and starting games and changing the rules and being the most fun funny Zofia they've ever seen. Mo says *what was on your cornflakes this morning* and I growl.

TOM

After school we go to the beach. I know Zofia doesn't want me to come and I don't want to go with her either. The look she gave me this morning was frightening and it's hanging between us and crackling in the air. I know she hates me. It feels like there's a thread between us that is constantly being pulled and tightened and soon it will snap. But Mum is at the hospital for an appointment and Marek is at the hospital working. I don't want to go back to the sloping cottage and sit alone while the day dissolves. But I also want to be far away from Zofia and Zofia will be on the beach.

But then Cameron and Halima and Jacob and Jude run after me when the last bell goes. *Not going home are you* yells Halima and Jacob tells me he's got a spare packet of crisps if I want them and Cameron wants us to do our homework together. These little voices start to sound louder than Zofia's and louder than the one in my head that says she's right. I nod slowly and Jude high-fives me and we all walk together in a group.

I pull off my shoes and socks and jumper and I rush into the waves. They are calmer than this morning. They wrap around me like an old friend and I make myself arrow sharp and straight and dive into the depths. The water is cold and it whips my breath from my chest but when I crack the waves apart and gulp air from the cloudless sky I don't feel better. I don't feel fixed and fresh and new.

I shake myself off just like Pablo does and I stamp over the sand and I see the huddle of them all on the beach. Halima and Leo are squabbling about volley-ball net heights and the markings Leo has been drawing in the sand and I don't want to get involved but they don't even ask for my input when I pass by. I keep going until I reach the main group of Ceto Class and I'm all ready with a smile and a joke and to slip right into the centre of everything. But they're joking and laughing and chucking a ball between them and Tom is grinning that rare grin. They don't even notice me and Jude says *that's absolutely hilarious, mate* to Tom and the storm inside me starts to rumble.

TOM

The sea is bright today. Far out towards the inky horizon are little licks of white foam that mirror the lazy clouds above them. The salt tangs my tongue. I am starting to get used to the rush and call and cry of the sea. I feel hypnotised by it.

We start the volleyball game after a while. I am on the same team as Zofia because I took her place yesterday and Jude says there's no point swapping out now. But even though I am playing with the same people and against the same people, it is a very different game today. Zofia is rough and fast and good. She wants to win. She can jump so high that her fingertips brush the clouds. She can leap across the sand in one quick swandive. Her shouts scatter the seabirds.

The ball sails through the blue air towards me. I lift

my curled fist and I am ready to strike. It is getting closer.

And closer.

And closer.

A roar.

A rush of saltwind and a dark shadow whooshing.

A blur.

A thump.

And the sea is the sky and the sky is the sea and everything is upside down.

There is cold sand in my mouth. I spit grit and it is cherry red.

The world is still tipped and spinning but there are people suspended the wrong way up above me. Dommo. Cameron. Jude. More footsteps and more faces.

Bleeding

Bit rough that, Zo

Is he alive

Should we get your dad

It was his ball you know, Zofe

His eyes are open is that good?

I sit up and cough the beach from my lungs. Ceto Class seem to breathe out as one and Jacob or maybe Jude says *he's not dead!* which is a bit unnecessary. But then I don't feel quite alive. It's like I'm watching them from far away. I shake my head and the world lurches and spins and then rights itself.

Only Zofia is standing back. Her cheeks are pink but she's folded her arms tightly. *It was my ball* she mutters *he should have got out of the way. He was in the way*.

ZOFIA

Dommo helps Tom home. I stamp behind. It's not my fault he can't play volleyball. It's not my fault he was standing right there when I needed to get to the ball. It's not my fault he didn't move in time. It's not my fault he doesn't listen. It's not my fault he's so stickthin and tiny and birdboned that even the slightest shove sends him spinning. It's not my fault he bit his lip and bled everywhere. I don't know why everyone is acting like it is.

Dad and Fiona are in the kitchen talking in quiet voices with their heads bent close together. They don't notice us stamping inside and when they finally see Tom they both do this ridiculous gasp. They work in a hospital, honestly. I would have thought they'd have seen some blood before. It's only a little bit anyway. Barely a splash. A thimbleful. It has dripped on to Tom's sweater and bloomed into rock-pool patterns that are actually quite cool. I think I'd quite like a split lip to be honest but Tom doesn't like it at all. He doesn't cry though which surprises me. Dommo even told him he was brave as she was helping him home which is just about the maddest thing I have ever heard in my entire life.

Dad tries to look at Tom's lip but he pulls away like a mummy's boy and only lets Fiona see. She is sitting with one hand curled around her stomach and when she stands up she winces. Honestly. It is *not* that bad. He still has all of his teeth. I think.

She opens his mouth ever-so-gently like he's made of glass and not flesh and blood and bone like the rest of us. She shines her little doctor's pen torch and his mouth glows scarlet. *It's fine, my darling, it just needs a little rinse with some salt water and we'll put a tissue on it to stop the blood, OK? It might sting a little bit but that's good. It means the salt is cleaning it. OK? What happened?*

Tom says something and his words are a whisper that flutters and scatters and he says he tripped playing on the beach and I am almost impressed because I thought for sure he'd dob me in. Fiona nods and goes to the sink to sort some salt water and tissues and I can feel Dad looking right at me.

Fiona asks me if I'm all right too and I growl at her and tell her to leave me alone and Dad takes a deep breath. But he doesn't shout at me to go to my room. He breathes in the air around us like he's drowning and he says *sit down, we have something to tell you two*.

TOM

There's something wrong with the baby.

I knew before they said it. I knew before Mum wobbled out the words and changed the air around us. I knew. There's a moment before bad news settles around you like dust. I know that moment like I know the folds of a paper bird.

The baby might die.

I don't understand how something can die before it's even lived. How something that was so certain could be slipping away.

I don't understand any of it.

They found a problem yesterday on the scan. They went back today to hear how bad it is. And it's bad. So bad that they used words like *chances of survival* and *big operation* and it was like all their doctor language had suddenly become sharper and crueller because it was about them now. I think of the fluttering floating picture of my baby brother or sister and how I'd traced the lines of bone and thought how perfect everything looked in blurry black and white.

The baby might die.

ZOFIA

When Dad says the words I don't know what to do with them so I scrunch them up and push them down inside me. I can feel them wriggling though, wriggling and squirming in my belly. I jump up and down to try to make them stop and Dad says *what are you doing, Zofia, did you hear me?*

I nod and I go and I switch on the TV and watch a stupid cartoon that I haven't liked since I was six. I stare at the acid colours until they blur and swim but I don't say anything and I hear the others crying in the kitchen. I swallow down sick and words and sorrys.

The baby might die.

Wishes on the waves can come true.

TOM

Mum holds me. I can feel the bump between us and for a moment I am so angry with the baby that it ripples under my skin and she holds me even tighter. All my worry is tingling and stretching and yawning inside me. The baby. Mum. Us.

And Zofia didn't even care at all. I hate her. I hate her noise and her movements and the way she makes me feel when I'm around her. I hate the way she talks to Mum. I hate her. I hate her more than I hate what's happening. I hate her so much that every gristle and sinew inside me burns with it.

I hear her in her bedroom and she's shouting and crashing about and I want with all of my whole sad and angry heart for things to be different. The force of my wish hits me like a cannonball because I didn't think that this would be the thing I wanted most in the world. It's like an electric shock. A power surge that trembles to the ends of my fingers and sparks around me. A darkness inside me that roars.

I wish that Zofia would disappear.

I make paper cranes all night with the lights on but the darkness creeps through the cracks in the floor and crawls inside me.

ZOFIA

In the morning Dad tries to talk to me about *operations* and *outcomes* and *supporting each other* but I don't listen. He tells me he knows it's a shock but I still don't say anything. I haven't got anything to say. He keeps talking and he keeps looking at me and he keeps leaving space for my words so I say

If the baby dies will Tom and Fiona leave?

And that sick twisty feeling in my tummy roars back into life as Dad's face drains to paperwhite.

TOM

Mum and I go for a walk on the beach and it's just the two of us. The whole world seems wide and open across the swirling sea but at the same time I feel cocooned by the curve of the cliffs.

I haven't had proper time alone with Mum for ages. I want to tell her how worried I am about her and how I can't sleep at all without every single light on, not even for five seconds, and how I'm folding a thousand paper cranes for the chance of just one wish and how worried I am about the baby nestled alone in the dark. But I can't find the words and I can't let her know that I'm crumbling like the cliffs. So I tell her about school and volleyball and Cameron and she tells me about work and a book she's reading and she asks me lots of questions too. The wind twists our hair into salty tangles and she laughs and says I need a haircut which is true.

We walk down to the inky edge of the sea and she finds smooth pebbles for us to skim. At first I'm rubbish but she shows me just how to hold the stone and keep it flat and how to flick my arm so that it skips across the water like a pondskater. It feels like the beach has carried us to a whole other world that's just for us. I feel myself relax into the rhythm of finding stones and streaking them across the water.

We count each flickery jump and shout the numbers into the sky. I get eight and Mum gets nine. *It's beautiful here, isn't it* she says and I nod because it is. I hold Mum's hand because Zofia isn't here to laugh and I whisper *everything will be OK?* and I don't mean to put a question mark on the end but I do. And Mum squeezes my hand and she says she doesn't know but she hopes so. Hope is all there is. Then she takes my hand and rests it on the curve of her tummy and I feel skimming stones on the sea. Flickery jumps. Hope.

The sun is starting to melt into the sea and my fingers are getting stiff with cold when I realise we're late. We're late for tea and Marek is cooking and my heart starts to tremble. The food will go in the bin and there will be shouting and darkness. I look at Mum and she's finding more pebbles and I tug her hand and say *we have to go back.*

Mum walks slowly and the whole way I chew the inside of my cheek until I taste the metal tang of blood. When we get inside the cottage I am coiled tight like a spring. Marek sticks his head out of the living room and says *ah there are the windswept walkers – your tea is in the oven to keep warm. Tom, do you want apple or orange juice?*

ZOFIA

The days are getting longer. In every single possible sense because the sun is getting up earlier and earlier and bathing the sea in gold and also because living with Tom and Fiona makes time seem like it's in a coma.

Dad isn't really talking to me. Tom never talks to me. Fiona does but I don't care. The baby is maybe going to die.

I didn't know it could be so boring when things are also so terrible. You expect when everything is bad and wrong and awful that every single moment is lit up like a firework. But actually all that happens is I go to Dommo's house every day for tea after volleyball on the beach. I don't say a word to her about the baby or what I wished. I keep that curled up inside me. Tom spends most of his time with

Cameron doing maths or something. Who knows. Who cares. Dad probably does, actually. I don't think he's looked right at me properly since I said what I said. Even though he asks me if I'd like ice cream for pudding or tells me to hang up my coat or asks if I want to watch TV just like normal, it's not really like normal.

Dommo and I go swimming. It's May so not quite warm enough not to wear wetsuits but it's not so cold that our lips stain blue. The sand is shaking off its grey and gold is peeking through. I practise my lazy front crawl against the waves. My times haven't got much better over the past few months. Every time I get close to Fiji something seizes in my muscles and my brain and my skin and I have to turn back and splash to the shore. Dommo says it's cramp and I should eat a banana but obviously I'm not going to do that.

I strike the water again and again and I'm no longer lazy but stretching and twisting and pulling myself through the current. I can do this I can break through I can swim against the tide and scrabble my way on to the biting rocks of Fiji and plant the flag I made that's hiding in my wetsuit pocket. Then whenever I sit on the shore I'll be able to see the greying saltsplashed outline of Pablo's face fluttering on its bright orange cloth.

Then my breath catches in my chest again. My legs start to scream. The pain doubles and twists and pierces itself through me like bolts of lightning. I gasp and swallow the sea. Every time I kick I see a flash of Dad. A flash of Tom and Fiona. A flash of the baby. I paddle with my hands to keep myself afloat and I struggle and swim and I struggle and swim and struggle and swim until I can flop down on the shore and lie gasping and gaping like a fish.

It keeps happening. It's like my body isn't my own and the sea doesn't belong to me any more. In all the weeks and months since they arrived I haven't got a stroke nearer to Fiji. I used to be the best swimmer in the whole of the entire universe, or at least Ceto. I thought I'd have this sewn up months before the big summer beach school when all the slowcoaches finally manage it. And now here I am, writhing like a stranded eel on the sand while Dommo kicks calmly through the water and gets closer and closer to my goal.

TOM

Now that there's bad news that hangs like a storm-cloud around our shoulders, I am just waiting. I'm waiting for the thunder to roar and for the lightning to strike. I spend all night waiting, counting seconds and counting paper cranes. I can't have the lights off at all and even with them on the floorboards ooze darkness and my heart skips beats. I can't get rid of the darkness. Zofia spends all her time at the beach or in the bath and every time I see her I think about the box of birds and my wish. I push down thoughts of other things I could wish for and I polish this wish until it shines.

I have waited and waited for Marek to snap. When Mum is late or when the hospital calls with news about the baby or when I don't hear him calling me for tea or when Zofia is rude or when Pablo is sick on the floor after stealing toast. I wait because I know sometimes the snap can come much later than you expect. Sometimes it can be right away and sometimes it can take days and so you always have to be prepared. But it's been weeks. Weeks and weeks and there's been nothing. Not a shout or a slap or a clicked lock and darkness.

There's been homemade Polish sourdough bread and suppers cooked together and walks on the beach with the dog and nights watching films with popcorn and hot chocolate and tears about what might happen with the baby and hugs to try to make it better just for a moment.

Sometimes I forget that I'm waiting.

They spend their time as a family and I spend my time in the waves and counting seconds in the bath. I sometimes wonder if I'm really one of those part-seal selkie children and I should just make my life at sea instead of in the cottage. I examine my skin for signs of seal and it's just puckered from the salty water. But I don't fit in at home any more and I can't swim like a selkie so I am caught in between and it makes me rage.

I want the sea to hold me. I want it to keep me in one piece so when I dip my head below the waves I can't think about all the things that are racing loudly round my brain. I want to be where there's just sealight and quiet. But at the moment the sea whirls me round and spits me out on the shore in the roaring wind.

TOM

I don't see a lot of Zofia but Marek and I have started to walk Pablo together and I don't feel the same flit of panic when we're alone together. It's there but it isn't all of me. Zofia doesn't come because she's always disappearing down to the beach and coming back soaking wet and spitting sand and salt and looking like fury.

I also have a friend. Or maybe friends. I'm not sure. Ceto Class goes to the beach every day after school and we play volleyball and tig and some of them swim, especially as it's getting warmer. Everyone sticks together and even when there are little arguments everyone is friends again quick as a flash. The arguments usually involve Zofia and a goal she is certain should or shouldn't be allowed. But Cameron and I sit together and talk about maths and science and stories. He is quiet and kind and he doesn't call me a freak when I tell him about folding paper or making lights or about the baby or even about Dad. I don't tell him why I need lights or why I fold paper or about the Incident at my last school but I do tell him where Dad is. And he doesn't shout it out to Ceto Class or shuffle a bit further away from me or say he has to go home. He says *that must be really hard for you* and I look at him in surprise because I've folded that feeling away for a long time, but it is hard for me. It really is.

It's the May Regatta at the weekend which basically means we all get to go to the harbour and eat ice cream and watch a load of fancy expensive boats sailing up and down and showing off their sails. I love the regatta, usually because Dad and I always go and we always have at least three scoops in every cone and I get chocolate sauce if I want it. I like watching the boats too even if they're a bit silly and I like the noise and the push of the crowds.

Obviously I'm not looking forward to it this year because this year we're bringing Fiona who is getting bigger before my very eyes and Tom who will probably hide under a barrel if anyone says hello to him. And I'm the only one who isn't constantly looking like they might cry. If they start crying when we're all out in public I will have to jump in the sea.

Ceto Class are all going and this year they're even keener than usual because Jacob and Jude's big brother Nathan is going to be sailing and we all think he might let us on his boat for a bit. I let my mind wander and think about what might happen if Nathan was suddenly taken ill while we were all aboard and I was the only one who could captain us back to shore and how maybe I might have to steer us round vicious rocks ready to scrape their teeth across our hull and battle a giant sea snake and everyone in the harbour would be cheering as I sailed us triumphantly back to safety and I'd be a hero.

When we arrive it's chaos and it's brilliant. Gulls are screeching and circling and trying to steal people's pasties and chips. Bunting has been strung up all through the little cobbled streets and round the harbour and it's like a springtime Christmas. I see Dommo and dash off towards her with Pablo at my heels but Dad grabs my arms and says *take Tom with you today please, Zofia* and I shake him off and glare but he doesn't take it back. *Go on* he says and I give a growl of annoyance and Pablo barks back. Tom doesn't look much like he wants to come with me but he looks at Fiona and she nods and says *have fun* and so that's that then.

TOM

The harbour is so busy and crowded that I want to turn around and run all the way back to the cottage. Even if it means being alone. I scan every face in the crowd and I can feel my heart starting to drum. I am a hawk watching and watching but I'm not hunting. I feel like I'm the prey.

I don't want to leave Mum but Zofia drags me down towards the water where Dommo and Cameron and Leo and Halima are already waiting. Next to them is a shiny boat with a great blue curved sail that is stretching itself against the wind. Jacob or possibly Jude sticks his head out of a cabin onboard and shouts *all right, guys, check out my boat* and Leo chucks a bit of pasty at him. A seagull immediately swoops down and grabs it nearly before it's even left Leo's hand and I duck. Zofia laughs and the sound is whipped up by the sails and rises above the clamour of the sea.

Nathan lets us come onboard under the very strict instructions that if we touch anything or break anything or breathe on anything or basically move at all he will quite happily sling us into the sea. He eyes Pablo with extreme suspicion, which is fair enough because he's already secretly done a little wee at the front of the boat but that's going to get wet anyway, surely. Tom offers to stay on dry land with Pablo but there is absolutely no way I am leaving my dog with him. He'd probably drop the lead the second a seagull flapped nearby and that would be the end of that.

The boat is very cool. I love the way it's like standing on the waves. The floor rolls backwards and forwards and the sea sprays in my hair and the horizon calls to me. I want to sail away. We're meant to learn to do a bit of sailing this summer on the beach and I've done a bit before when I was little but I was always much more about the whole swimming thing. But this is brilliant and I tell Nathan I want to come with him. He laughs and says *not a chance, little one, you wouldn't last a minute* and I burn because I am not little and I'm tougher than he is I bet. I spin on my heel which is actually quite hard to do on a small boat and storm off and smack bang into Tom. He is always there. Always in the way and I scream at him to move and I don't care that Ceto Class are staring.

TOM

I jump out of the way and Zofia stalks past me trailing a stormcloud and Pablo. I feel my cheeks bloom with hot blood and I look down at the sea and it makes me feel sick so I look up at the sky.

You all right, mate, she's just a hothead yeah says Leo and I nod. *You wanna see downstairs* shouts Jacob and Leo says *come on let's have a look then* and I don't really want to leave the safety of the open sky but I do anyway.

The stairs are tiny and narrow. I put my arms out and keep my hands flat on the cool walls as I climb slowly down the stairs. I am behind Leo and Cameron and if I trip I will break us all. Cameron's body is blocking a lot of my view down but it looks dark. I feel for my torch in my pocket and my fingers meet soft seams and fluff. I grope around blindly and my trembling hands pull frantically at nothing. I haven't got it. I see it suddenly in a flash in my mind, sitting patiently on my desk, waiting to be moved from my school trousers to my jeans. I forgot. I'm so stupid. I forgot. After what happened at Treverton I swore I would never ever be without a torch again and now I'm going down into the dark and it's all happening all over again.

ZOFIA

I see Leo and Jacob and Cameron and Tom all disappear down a set of narrow stairs. Without me. Dommo and Halima are here and Alma and Mo have just arrived and Nathan is halfway up the sail doing something strange with ropes but the boys have just left me. I would have liked to see downstairs but they chose stupid Tom. The anger that has been sparking under my skin since Nathan wouldn't let me sail with him starts to catch fire. The anger that has been flickering since Tom first arrived. The anger that has been smouldering since the bad news about the baby. They all catch fire together and I burn with them. I storm over to the tiny open door that leads to the stairs and with a flare of fury I slam it shut and I slide the bolt across.

TOM

I hear the door slam and I think it's the wind until the scrape of a bolt echoes down the stairs. I freeze. We are standing in the dark belly of the boat and there are no lights on. The tiny window of light at the top of the stairs is swallowed in a second and then it is all around me. The creeping shadows. The shapes that grow and twist and reach and there's a growling hum in the air. The dark blooms and spreads and I try to blink it away and I'm blinking and trembling and I know I'm starting to cry too because my face is damp. I haven't let myself be in the whole darkness since we moved here and I've forgotten how to breathe it away. I gulp more and more air but there will never be enough and my breath is coming in sharp bursts that burn my chest and my heart is thundering so fast that it will soon explode and I'm going to die I'm going to die I'm going to die and I am back in the room where he used to put me when I was bad and when I made trouble and I'm alone all alone in the black and I'm going to die I'm going to die I'm going to die.

Then there is a sudden burst of brightness. Light floods into me like a shockwave. Light pushes out the dark and forces it scuttling back into corners. Light shows me everything that was hidden before. A small room with a tiny table and a little sink. A lot of boxes and wires I don't understand. A humming fridge. Three faces staring at me and Leo has his finger on a light switch on the wall.

ZOFIA

Obviously I unlock the door after about three seconds and after Dommo has shouted at me in quite an unDommo-like way. It really wasn't a big deal. They would have spent the same amount of time down there even if I hadn't shut the door so I don't know why everyone is making such a fuss. Cameron is the first to emerge and at first I think he's walking like a crab either because we're on a boat and he's taking that seriously or because he's caught some terrible crab condition from the seawater. But actually he's moving sideways up the stairs so he can support Tom. Tom who isn't able to get up the steps on his own. Tom who is ghost glowing and trembling from every fibre of every muscle in his body. I've heard the phrase shaking like a leaf before but I've never really understood it because leaves are paper-thin and fragile and people are tough with bone and muscle and all the gristle that holds us together. But Tom is shaking like a leaf. It's like he's been flattened and hollowed out and he's quivering in the wind.

What on earth happened down there I mutter and Jacob emerges and says *the door slammed shut and all the lights were off*. I laugh because I thought something really awful must have happened to Tom but Cameron throws me a glance that burns my skin. I've never seen him look so furious.

Why's he shaking so much just because of a door shutting and a bit of dark whispers Dommo and Halima looks to me like I have the answers. I laugh like a hyena and I am about to say something a bit rude but Cameron glares at all of us and Dommo and Halima go bright red.

Cameron keeps whispering to Tom and the words are soft and gentle and kind and Tom is glass-eyed and damp-faced and his fingers are fluttering and he is sucking air in sharp whistles through white lips.

I don't know what to do. I look back at Dommo and Halima but Halima is now rubbing Tom's back and

Dommo is rustling her pockets until she finds a packet of sweets which she holds out for the shock and why is everyone acting like this is just a normal way to be when you get trapped in the dark and why is everyone paying him all this special attention and why is everyone looking at me like I'm some kind of monster?

Nathan swings himself down from his sail and he sits Tom down and he says *OK, mate, breathe in through your nose and out through your mouth, that's right, in through the nose out through the mouth, keep doing that, it's just panic OK it's just panic and you can breathe it away* and then he tells everyone to give Tom some space and I think he's taken all of mine away from me anyway. I jump off the boat and on to the harbour and Pablo and I sit and watch as Tom throws up over the side.

TOM

I feel a bit better once I've been sick. Except now there's sick all down the side of Nathan's boat and Nathan was so kind to me. I wait to see if his mood will flip and turn itself inside out and burst like fireworks from inside him but he doesn't even seem to notice. He gets me some water and I sip it slowly and try to wash the taste out of my mouth.

Ceto Class are hovering in the background and there is a low murmur passing through them like the buzzing of bees. I can't look up. I can't look at them. I can't meet their eyes now they know how pathetic I am. No one else down in that boat's belly was scared. No one else let all their breath escape and couldn't catch it back again. No one else was sick off the side of the boat. I can still hear Zofia's laugh bouncing off the waves.

I just want to go home.

I was so stupid to think this wouldn't happen again.

Obviously Dad and Fiona are going to notice there's something wrong with Tom because he's green-gilled and shaking. He rushes off the boat without saying a word to anyone and speeds away from the harbour like Pablo after a rabbit. I hare after him because if I lost him Dad would kill me and unlike Pablo he's not microchipped. I follow him through the crowds and tangles of legs and bags and dog leads and shouts of *oi* and *watch it* and *careful* and *slow down*.

I am running out of oxygen when he comes to a grinding halt and I smack straight into his back and he goes down like the leaf he is and I land on top of him. I leap up like a scalded cat and Tom scrambles to his knees which are decorating his jeans with blossoms of blood. I am aware that this is the second time I've smashed into him and made him bleed and that this doesn't exactly look good but he doesn't even seem to notice the red stains spreading through blue denim. I offer him a hand to help him up but he ignores it and drags himself to his feet and limps off towards the pasty stall where Dad and Fiona are queuing.

Dad is furious with me when we get home. It's the kind of white-hot fury I haven't ever felt from him before, not even after I said that thing about the stupid baby. Now it shimmers from him in waves. He's not cross with me because I locked Tom downstairs on the boat because he doesn't know I did that and Tom doesn't know I did that and maybe Dommo knows but she hasn't said a word. He's furious with me because I am too rough and too loud and I'm not kind to Fiona or Tom and I've shoved him over twice and I don't take part in family life any more and I don't care about anyone but myself and I'm not behaving myself and he's fed up with it and the words wash over me like the tide and the salt of them rubs me raw. I can feel myself starting to crack and crumble under the weight of them and I stare back out to sea and I see Fiji stretching itself towards the sky and I whisper *I hate him I hate him I hate him*.

TOM

I have hot cocoa and Mum and I sit together and watch stupid TV and chat about stupid things. I didn't tell her what happened on the boat. I don't want to worry her and I can keep it inside. Marek is on the beach with Zofia and for a little while it feels exactly like it used to when it was just us. Except for Mum's bump. And the worry. And Pablo snoring on the rug. And the roar of the sea. But it's nice.

When Zofia stomps in without Marek Mum asks if she'd like to feel the baby kick. Zofia's face clouds and she doesn't even answer before she stamps her way up the stairs. *She's so horrible about the baby* I whisper before I can stop the words because I am trying to be good and kind. Mum strokes my hair and she says *she's just scared like we all are, Tom* and I laugh because there is nothing Zofia is scared of in the whole wide world.

I manage four seconds before the water streams the wrong way towards my brain and I cough and splutter my way out of the depths of the bath. I float there in the cold and I wonder what it would be like to feel the baby kick. I think about whether it would feel like a tickle or a thump against the palm of my hand. Then I stop myself. I put a padlock on the thoughts and I throw away the key. I don't want to know anything about the baby. I don't want to wonder.

TOM

At bedtime I still feel raw and turned around and upside down by today. I can feel a loud beat of shame tapping inside my ribs. Ceto Class are going to know I'm a freak and a weirdo and all the words the boys at my old school would use. All the words Dad would use. He'd say them after he had put me in the dark and locked the door. He'd open it after an hour or a minute or a second and I never knew which it was really. At first I didn't cry at all. But then the dark around me started to change. It would reach for me. It would hide things. It would bite and snap. It would hiss and whisper. And then he would open the door and the light would stream in all around me. He would stand in the mouth of it and he would laugh and I would just try to keep breathing.

At Treverton Primary George and Connor locked

me in the PE cupboard because they thought it would be funny. They thought it would make everyone laugh at me and laugh with them and it did both those things. They unlocked the door when my screaming got so loud they thought a teacher might hear and the laughter faded into silence and shock and horror. I tumbled out from the black mouth of the cupboard and into the streaming light. I curled in a ball on the floor. My fingers were bleeding from scratching at the door and there was a damp patch on my grey trousers. I wouldn't talk and I couldn't talk and I wouldn't move and I couldn't move. Macy ran to get the nurse. They had to call Mum in the end. She brought new trousers in and took me home but I wouldn't say what had happened. After that, no one at Treverton Primary talked to me. I was the screaming bleeding boy who wet himself because of the dark. No one wanted to be my friend. And it's going to happen all over again. Zofia laughed at me and it made me hate her.

I keep the lights on and I put squares of paper over the cracks in my floor to try to block out the darkness but I know it's still there and I can't make it go away. I make forty-seven paper cranes and all I can think about is the cardboard box that is filling up with bright birds and how soon I'll have enough and soon I can make my wish. It's a thought that's dark and bitter but it tastes good and I don't care and it makes me smile. I only stop folding when my fingers ache but I don't sleep until the sky is streaking pink with the morning and I've watched the sea change its light.

The next morning the birds start shouting their silly heads off and telling me to wake up. I growl at them because I want a lie-in because it's Sunday. I don't actually want to sleep because that's boring. I want to make my duvet into a tent and raid my secret underbed snack box and read the graphic novel Leo lent me last week. He stole it from his big brother and I think it has loads of cool things in it like zombies and vampires and swords that can chop through dragon skin. My snack box has a Crunchie, a Snickers, a packet of Hula Hoops, a candy bracelet and a chocolate eyeball left over from Halloween. I think there might also be an apple in there but it probably looks like the eyeball by now. It's been a while since I opened the box.

I get my snacks from their secret hiding place

under the squeaking floorboard near the foot of my bed. That's where I put all my best things, like chocolate and books Dad would say I'm too young to read. I'm on page six of my book and chocolate bar number two when Dad knocks on my door and pokes his face in and the new morning has burned off his bad mood with me.

Come on, up and dressed. I've got a surprise for you.

I love surprises. Unless they're surprise babies but they can't do that one again now. I jump up and pull on my jeans and a striped T-shirt with a parrot on it and I race down to the kitchen.

Tom is also there and he's stroking Pablo's lovely ears and he's dressed too. He doesn't look very happy to see me which is ridiculous because he doesn't actually know what I did and when I think about it I feel something uncomfortable and squirmy in my tummy. He's wearing shorts and his knees are scraped and raspberry red and I can see the shadow of a bruise on his chin. I turn to Dad but he's busy finding his wellies and also trying to swallow a mug of coffee and eat a croissant and feed the cat. He puts the croissant in Frida's bowl by mistake and I'm waiting for him to start accidentally munching on Fishie Treatz but he shakes the sleep from his head and opens the door. *Come on then* he shouts and Pablo scrabbles after him leaving Tom's hand scratching the air.

I follow my dog and my dad and I don't look back but I can hear Tom behind me.

TOM

I don't really want to go but Mum came into my room this morning. She sat on the end of my bed and she told me how proud she was of me and how Marek had something really fun planned that she thought I'd really like and how she'd be minutes away. She said I deserved to do something nice with *everything that's been happening*. Those words felt heavy when she said them. She said she'd be folding baby clothes all morning and it would be the most boring thing in the universe. I wouldn't mind doing that too but I want to be good for her. I don't want to cause any trouble.

I follow Zofia and Pablo and Marek out of the front door and shut it carefully behind me. It's the kind of fresh morning that we never got in the city. The sun is burning the clouds from the sky and the grass is damp with dew. The sea breeze tickles and I can see everything. I can see where the sea meets the sky and I can see the cottages that clutter the cliffs and I can see the road that winds through them. I can see the roof of the school and I can see the inky blur of the little island that sits in the middle of the waves.

Marek is walking towards what Mum called the stables when we first arrived here. There are no horses there now but there used to be when the cottage was first built. Now they're just grey crumbling stone buildings that have been battered and whipped by the sea winds and a century of storms. There is ivy winding its way around the walls and windows dark with dust. Marek is unlocking the doors and I'm worried that the whole thing might collapse on our heads.

He flicks a light switch and the light floods through my eyes and spreads all the way through my brain, so for a second I can't see a thing. Then shapes start to form. Lumps and lines. Dust motes spin and dance through the air. Even though my eyes have adjusted to the flood of sharp light I still can't quite understand what I'm seeing.

Is that says Zofia *half of a really terrible boat?*

It is. It is half of a really terrible boat. We learned about evolution last year and this boat looks like it is in the very first stages. All boats came from this boat. And they changed and got better. A lot better.

Dad is running his fingers along the bare ribs that I think are meant to be the hull. There is nothing connecting them so it's like a skeleton. A ghost ship. It even has silver spiderwebs stretching between its bones. I imagine undead pirates sailing it out on a misty sea with their zombie parrots screeching on their shoulders.

I started building this before you were even born, Zofia. I had these dreams about taking you sailing every summer. Messing about on the beach and learning to row. Heading out to the cove. Picnics and fishing, that sort of thing. But then your mum died when you were so tiny and work was so busy and I just left it here. Rotting away. But you two, you two are old enough to take over. We can build it all together. I can teach you but it's not so tricky, you know. You'll be able to do most of it yourselves once you have the basics, I think. It'll be, what do you call it? A project. A joint project.

I think the best thing for this boat is for it to be gently put out of its misery. Perhaps in the wood burner. The idea of doing a project with Tom makes my insides turn themselves over. I don't want to be stuck in this gloomy shed with him for hours and endless hours. I'd rather put my head in the wood burner. I'd rather shave off my eyebrows. I'd rather have to squawk like a chicken instead of talking. I'd rather be turned into a hamster that was inside out. I'd rather do *fractions*.

Tom is looking from Dad to the boat. I expect him to be as horrified as I am and to mumble something about not really wanting to but thank you very much. Especially after how much he freaked out just being on a boat yesterday. But that thing is happening to his face again. It's coming alive. There is a light behind his eyes and his whole body is turning from frozen to feathers.

There's no way he's getting to do a project with Dad without me.

I'm the captain I shout before I can stop myself.

TOM

I like building things. I like starting with nothing and ending up with something. I like taking things that look useless and maybe on their own are useless and I like making them work. I like fixing things and making them brand new. I have built a radio and a lamp and a torch and a tiny wind chime and that clock for Mum and a thousand worlds from Lego and paper. I can fold paper into new shapes just from my head now. When Mum is sad I make her a bird or an elephant or a whale and it always starts as just a flat square. Which is kind of amazing. When I build things it's like I get pulled into a whole new world. I sink down deep into tiny details and everything else melts far away and that tangle of knotted fear loosens its grip. Just a bit.

I don't want to go sailing or sit in a boat on the

choppy seas or row towards the horizon. I don't want to ever get on a boat again after yesterday. But I do want to build one. I want to take these arcs and arches and swoops of wood and I want to make them work and be what they're supposed to be.

Even if it's with Zofia.

Even if she's the captain.

Dad won't let me be the captain which is ridiculous and also extremely annoying because Dommo has a captain's hat she could lend me and it would look really great with my yellow raincoat and shiny black wellington boots. Dad says we have to be *joint captains* but that's stupid for two reasons: firstly Dommo only has one hat and secondly who on earth would take orders from Tom?

Dad goes to make us cups of hot tea because that's what woodworkers need apparently. He asks Tom how he likes it and Tom says he doesn't know. How you can not know that is beyond me but Dad nods and he comes back with a clinking tray. On it are four of our usual glass mugs with metal handles. There's a steaming teapot and a little jug of milk and a plate of acidbright lemon slices and our old chipped sugar bowl that's decorated with blue seabirds. I chose that from a shop in Wales when Dad and I went on holiday and climbed a mountain right to the very top.

Dad pours the tea and he tells Tom that he has his black with sugar and lemon and I have mine with milk and we both drink from the glass cups. Then he makes Tom a black tea with sugar and lemon and a tea just like mine and Tom tastes both. *Let's find out if you're Polish or English in your heart* says Dad and it's quite funny really. Tom sips both like he's taking it very seriously which he probably is. He's probably got some sort of scientific scales and rating system and I wouldn't be surprised if he whips out a bar chart and one of those funny pointing sticks professors use. Dad and I wait like it's a competition to see whose tea is the best which I suppose it is actually. Tom takes his time and he goes back and tries them both again and I am hopping like a frog with burned toes. *Come on come on come on which one* I chant and Tom grins in that way that takes me by surprise sometimes and he says *I'm sorry, Marek, but your tea is completely disgusting*.

This might be the most I have ever heard him speak and I jump up and down and crow and dance around the stable saying *I told you so* and Dad laughs so much I think he might choke.

Tom laughs too and so do I and the fury of yesterday and of all the other million days melts a little bit in the tea-stained steam of the stable.

TOM

Building a boat is a lot harder than making a fish from a piece of paper. Marek has already built the bones which he says is the hard bit but it all seems quite hard. He teaches me and Zofia how to plane wood, which means running a tool called a planer across a piece of wood to shape it and smooth it. He makes it look easy. He pushes the planer and it glides under his careful hand. When I do it I gouge a chunk out of the wood in a jaggedy line. I stop and I'm horrified because I've ruined it like I ruin everything. I wait for the shouting and hands and the whirl of the world as I'm pushed into the dark. Panic crashes through me and I close my eyes and wait. But it doesn't happen.

Marek says *that's good, you're getting the hang of it, that first bit was really smooth. You just need to move your hand with the wood, see?* And he is about to put his hand over mine to show me but then he stops and says *Zofia, come here and Tom can copy*. And he puts his hand over hers and I copy the flow and rhythm of their movements.

And we go on, smoothing and planing and shaping a boat together in the stables while the morning slips away. I don't think about anything but the shape of the wood and my mind is empty and calm. Then Marek goes to sort out lunch and I am alone with Zofia. I don't look up and I keep my eyes on the wood in front of me but my fingers fumble and I slice the skin of my thumb. I try to keep the gasp of pain inside but it slips out and Zofia wanders over. I expect her to laugh or call me a baby or just ignore the cut completely but she doesn't do anything like that. She calmly opens a green plastic box that's sitting on one of the wooden benches and without a word she carefully washes the blood and dirt from the jagged cut with a squirt of sterile water from a small bottle and then she wraps a plaster around my thumb. Her hands are so slow and gentle that it's like she's a different person. She examines a smear of my blood that's stained her hand and says *it's lucky I'm not a vampire because I'm very hungry, let's go and have some lunch*.

We have lunch in the kitchen and I am covered in curls of wood and dust and dirt. My muscles are sharp and stinging and my blisters are printing circles on my fingers. Mum passes me a cheese toastie and asks me if I'm having fun and I say *yes*. And I am.

We build the boat all day. We don't stop until the night sky is starting to blow across the sea and our tummies are rumbling louder than the scrape of the tools. We stand back and look at what we've achieved and I'll be honest, it doesn't look like much. I know we weren't going to build a boat in a day but if possible we have gone backwards. In fact we've definitely gone backwards because after lunch Dad decided the way he'd built the boat twelve years ago is not how he'd build a boat now. I wanted to ask him how the last twelve years had suddenly transformed him into a modern boat-making expert but he had that faraway thinking look on his face so I don't think he'd have heard me even if I did. Anyway he made us start from scratch.

He helped us cut what will eventually be the flat

back end of the boat from a piece of plywood. Dad showed us how to use a saw and how to keep it level and flat so it didn't bite the wrong way and tear up the wood. It was extremely hard and I nearly sawed my whole arm off. It's an absolute miracle I survived. Tom made neat little cuts because of course he did.

I'm not exactly sorry to see the back of the Frankenboat but I am desperate to push our boat across the soft sand and row to faraway lands and catch fish for my supper and feel the waves rocking me and be a tiny speck with all the ocean to explore.

We sit around the table and eat freezer pizza and chips for supper which is my favourite ever meal. I put ketchup on everything until it looks like there's been a murder on my plate and then I add a bit more. Tom picks at his chips like a baby sparrow but he finishes more of his food than he did yesterday. Building a boat is hungry work.

When will it be done I ask Dad and he thinks and says *well, probably about the same time the baby arrives*. There's a little beat of silence because we all know what might come after that. Or before that.

I don't like measuring time using the baby but by my reckoning that means it'll take three months. *Three months!* We'll miss the whole of the summer. I stick out my tongue and tell him that that's unacceptable. I hear a little snigger and look at Tom but he's staring very hard at a chip. Dad shrugs and says that if we take it seriously and work hard after school then we might be able to get it done before the baby and I want him to stop saying that stupid word.

Right then I say and I hold a chip aloft like a bloody sword. *We're building that boat as fast as we can and sailing it as far as we can this summer*.

Fiona smiles at me and tells me I'm very *determined* which is a word that is often used to describe me and usually means I'm not listening to what anyone else is saying. But here I think she means it as a good thing and I feel a little rush of something warm. I turn to Tom and say *you in then* and there's a tiny pause and in that moment I feel like I'm falling down through space and I want to shout that I don't care I'll do it on my own but then he nods and I eat my chip like I wasn't bothered anyway.

Before the sun slips down to the sea I swim with Dommo. She flips on to her back to watch the gold-painted sky and she says *did you shut him down there, Zo* and I shake my head from side to side so fast that I flick pearls of seawater in an arc around us. *He's just a wimp* I say and she gives me a funny look and glides away.

I am too full of chips to swim very far but I kick and splash and try to stretch the burn from my legs when it arrives. Fiji floats on the horizon and it's a million miles away.

TOM

The Sunday night after we start building the boat Zofia disappears down to the sea again and I am alone again.

I only make four paper cranes. They feel less important tonight. The need for the wish and the shout of my panic are both quieter. Every time the panic starts to twist and climb I think about how to clamp a piece of wood and how to hold a saw and how to pull it back and forth back and forth back and forth so its teeth don't snag and bite. The pull and push of the saw in my head matches the lap and whoosh of the waves outside my window and my heart stays slow for a little while.

The next morning there's no school because of an inset day. I'm glad. I don't want to see Ceto Class now that they know about me. For the first time I feel like

I've lost friends, because before when people realised what I was they weren't my friends anyway. I don't want to go to school and feel that something's disappeared. I want to stay in the stables and concentrate on shaping the swirls and grain of wood into something new.

I am eating buttered toast when Marek tells us we need supplies for building the new boat. Wood and glue and something called epoxy which is a special glue, and clamps to hold it all together because the old ones are bleeding rust. We'll need varnish to seal it against the salty water and that means we can choose whether to stain it dark or light or perhaps paint it a colour. I want something light and Zofia wants something dark. We have an argument over breakfast that isn't really an argument because all that happens is I say I'd like light and she starts shouting. Marek tells her to pipe down or he'll throw her in the sea and that we'll choose a colour closer to the time.

We drive in Marek's car and I sit in the back because Zofia baggsies the front. I want Mum to come too but she's sorting a million things for the baby. The little yellow room changes every day. I like that it's being made just right but my heart tugs too because I don't know if there will ever be a baby in there now.

There's a white cot and a mobile of seabirds hanging from the ceiling. A thousand tiny outfits are tucked away in a chest of drawers. A little soft toy mole sits in the cot looking ready to burrow into the mattress. I thought the mole was a bit of an odd choice but Marek thought it was hilarious. It was that or a squid apparently.

Zofia doesn't like it when Mum or Marek mention the baby. They try to talk to her about what might happen when the baby's born. That it'll be poorly and it'll need an operation and we have to hope hope hope that it will work. But Zofia won't listen. She kicks her toes into the ground and her face is a stormcloud and her eyes flash like lightning. She's always so angry. It's like fire is burning just below her skin and ready to spark at any moment.

The car bumps and winds along the cliff roads and I feel a bit sick all over again. I used to get very carsick and Dad would get furious and say I'd ruined his seats and the smell and the stain would never come out. The first time he shouted about it Mum told him it wasn't my fault and that this is what happened when people like him drive too fast and brake too hard. I don't remember what happened after that. It's like my brain has cut out the memory and folded it up into a tiny square and tucked it away somewhere where I can't get to it. But I do know that Mum didn't ever tell Dad it was his fault again. She started making plans instead.

I take deep breaths and try to look at the fixed point on the horizon but it keeps moving as we twist down through the wild lanes. Marek looks at me in the mirror and his eyes meet mine for a flicker of a second. The next time we go round a bend it's much smoother and slower and my tummy stops rolling over.

The boatyard is incredible. It's different to the harbour with its sleek boats that could cut through the water like a knife and were just visiting for the day. Here everything has been here forever. It smells like tar and varnish and glue and the sea. There are groups of men with wind-whipped faces and salt-lined wrinkles running deep from the corners of their eyes. Their hands are red and rough and the skin is made from something different to mine. I can feel my heartbeat quicken and jump as they shout and bellow at each other through the seawinds. I watch them slapping sticky varnish on the sides of boats that have never touched the waves and sawing wood that will be made into something entirely new and I can't look away.

The boatyard is brilliant. There are tangles of ropes and sea-stinking lobster pots and jumbles of wood and nets and bright buoys nestled like jewels in the chaos. Beyond the yard is the wide open sea but it's crowded with a thousand fishing boats and they're bobbing and nodding on the waves. They're all painted different colours. Little shoals of red boats and green boats and yellow boats mixed with dark wood and light wood and white and blue. I can see careful curling script on the sides of some of them and I know that boats have names just like people.

Tom is stuck in place staring at all the fishermen with their hands knotted like old tree bark. Dad is already making his way to talk to them with a paper list flapping in the wind like a gull's wing. I bounce after him and Tom follows slowly. He steps so carefully. He picks his way through the splashes of oil and coils of rope and I knock over a metal bucket full of crabs. It's quite hard to get fifty crabs back into a bucket they didn't really want to be in in the first place but I manage it. Mostly. A few scuttle off under the upturned hulls of broken boats but really I've just given them a second chance.

TOM

We buy a lot of stuff. Huge sheets of plywood and tins of varnish and a nearly new saw. Marek borrows the other things we might need off a man called Saul. Saul knows a lot about how to build boats and he looks like he's built from the same stuff. He is knotted and stiff and varnished by the outdoors. He points out to sea with his calloused finger and shows us all the boats he's built. They bob and dip and catch the shine of the sun. Some of them have flickering sails, some of them are cluttered with fishing nets and some of them have little cabins with windows that peep out over the water. They're beautiful. I want to tell Saul that but I can't find my voice here. Zofia tells him and he grins proudly and says no one builds a proper boat any more. Then he gives us both a pound, which Marek makes us put in a charity tin collecting for lifeboats, and a horrible sweet that tastes of the inside of a pocket and of fish too.

Zofia and I have to help carry all of the things to the car. The wood burns my blistered hands and I understand why the fishermen's fingers are the way they are. It takes ages to tie everything with twists of blue rope to the roof of the car and by the end my hands are burning.

On the way home Marek takes the winding roads and the turns slowly. Zofia wants him to vroom like a racing driver but he just shakes his head and says it's because of all the wood lashed to the top of the car and he carries on. I feel like I'm torn in two again because I think I'm causing trouble and making things difficult but I don't want to be sick on the seats either. Zofia grumps and mutters darkly but by the time we pull up outside the cottage she's excited about boatbuilding. She changes her mood in a flash sometimes.

ZOFIA

We shift all of the new boat stuff into the stables. I'm still trying to spit the taste of Saul's pocket sweet out of my mouth. It's a lovely combination of fluff and varnish and dust and fish. It means I'm not much help with the really big bits of wood. But I recover enough to carry the clamps and glue and a handful of hammers and Dad and Tom do the rest. I'm quite surprised by Tom. He is so small but it's like there's an invisible force inside his muscles that means he can lift anything at all. His face is set and sweaty but he keeps going and when we stop he looks at his hands and they're blistered and bleeding. If this had happened to me I'd want chocolate for the shock and an emoji plaster but Tom just wipes them down on his trousers and walks towards the stables.

We have a snack of Oreos and orange juice and Tom eats his like they're an actual sandwich rather than prising them open and licking out the filling which is what any normal person would do. It's what I do. It's what Dommo does. I think about showing him how they taste so much better if you do it my way and especially if you dip them into your orange juice because then you've got a chocolate orange but he doesn't even look my way the whole time we're eating. I don't know why I bother.

We start on the boatbuilding again. Dad gives us quite a boring lecture on exactly what we're going to do and he shows us some paper plans that Saul gave him. I start to wander off in my mind and I'm imagining sailing away for a year and a day but not with an owl like in a poem my dad used to read to me. I'll take a dog and a pussycat and a year's supply of Oreos rather than a jar of honey because that's an extremely weird thing to take on an ocean voyage. I don't see why I'd need any money but I have thirty-two pounds and sixty-eight pence in my money box which is a lot more than a five-pound note. I'll take that too and I'll lie curled up in the bottom of my boat while the sea rocks me to sleep and the stars prick the sky.

TOM

Zofia is obviously not listening to anything Marek is saying but I am. I listen to every single word and I file them in my brain to get out and look at later. I follow his finger as he points at lines and dots and dashes on the paper Saul gave him. The lilt of his voice is so gentle. I am drawn in and absorbed and everything else fades away.

We need to build the flat back of the boat all over again. It's called the butt end which sends Zofia into hysterics. Then we need to build the sides and put a brace from one side to the other to give it strength. Then add the front. Flip it over and put the bottom on. All the seams that hold the boat together are going to be glued with a super-special waterproof glue. It sounds simple. And Marek keeps saying it is a very simple boat and it won't last forever but it's going to be brilliant. And I think it might be.

The boat will be magnificent. After a long day of sawing and learning some basic first aid as a direct consequence of the sawing, we have stitched the new butt end of the boat to the sides. Stitching is not with a needle and thread which was a huge relief to me but actually involves glue that smells like the inside of a fish and a lot of clamps to hold everything together. I wasn't at all neat with the glue and I nearly stuck myself to some wood but Tom noticed and pulled us apart before it could set and he only laughed just a tiny bit. He held the sides steady for me so I could dribble the glue along the edges and I very nearly managed to do it quite neatly after that.

I am hot and sticky and tired and I smell like fish and wood and hard work. I spring out of the stable door and head down to the beach before Dad can tell me to help clear up and wash gluey brushes and put everything away exactly where it belongs rather than just sensibly leaving it where it is so it's there for next time. I strip down to my pants and T-shirt and I plunge into the water.

I need to practise. Obviously I need to practise because I seem to be getting worse and worse every time I swim. But instead of trying to kick towards Fiji, I lie on my back and stare at the huge bright sky above me as the waves rock me from side to side. I have to kick occasionally or flap my arms so I don't tip up and over or end up spiked on some rocks but when I do that I don't feel the jellyfish sting or the crush of the sea on my lungs. I feel like I used to in the water. I feel calm.

There is a prickling on the back of my neck and I don't think it's a friendly hermit crab. It feels like eyes on me and I don't like it one bit because I came here to be on my own. I flip on to my front and look at the beach stretched out against the evening. Tom is standing on the sand toeing the water with a trainered foot. Pablo sees me and starts barking joyfully and splatters his way towards me spraying sand and water in spirals around him and covering Tom. I giggle and Tom definitely hears but it's very funny and then he gives a little smile and wipes the sand off his front with his blistered hands.

Come in I shout and I surprise myself again because why would I want him in my sea? But Tom shakes his head anyway and he shouts *I haven't got my stuff* and I throw my arms up in the air because I'm swimming in a parrot T-shirt and my pants and we also do happen to live about thirty seconds away. But I'm in a good mood because of the sea and the sky and the dog and the boat and so I paddle my way back to shore and I sit with him on the sand.

For a moment he looks like he might rather throw himself in the sea but when Pablo bounds back towards us and empties half of the ocean into our laps with one big shake Tom laughs and his face is light. I throw some kelp for Pablo and for a while we just sit in silence and watch the waves swallowing the sand little by little.

TOM

Even though the wind is whipping and the sea is storming and the gulls are screeching, there is a quiet here. Zofia sits next to me and she throws seaweed for Pablo and she gazes out towards the horizon and for once all of her thoughts aren't tumbling in a tangle from her head to her mouth. She hasn't even laughed at me for what happened on Nathan's boat yet, and it's been two days. I thought she would but she hasn't said a word. She mumbled a sulky sorry for smashing me on to the cobbles afterwards but she didn't say a single syllable about what happened when I burst into the light on the boat. I thought she'd laugh.

I like the silence we're sharing. I feel like something has moved between us. Like the tide is pulling and pushing us all the time but for now everything is flat and calm.

Zofia is staring at the little cluster of dark toothy rocks that peek monstrously from beneath the waves. The teeth are scattered with bright flags that follow the breaths of the wind. *What are they for* I ask her and I point towards them.

Oh. Just one little sound. *Just Fiji. The flags belong to people who swim there like you've conquered it, like you own a little bit of space there just for you. All yours.*

I look at the flags and it's like they're swimming against the sky. I wonder which one is Zofia's and I ask her and her face closes down lightning fast. A storm is brewing in her eyes again but she blinks and the dark clouds clear a little bit. She shrugs and says *haven't put one there yet, not really bothered. Doesn't matter does it. I'll do it this summer and most of us haven't even done it yet all right it's really far away* and the more she keeps talking the more I know it's the most important thing in the whole world to her.

ZOFIA

I wish I hadn't told him about Fiji. It's mine and it's one thing I didn't have to share with him and now he knows all about it. But somehow as the light fades the sky to a purple bruise and the sea blooms with evening colours I don't mind so much. We sit on the beach and we talk about the boat and how long it will take for glue to dry and shapes to be drawn and wood to be cut and it's not like talking to a strange scaredy-cat boy who stole my life but someone who is just part of it instead.

TOM

I only make five paper cranes before I fall asleep with just one light glowing to fight the darkness that crawls from the floor. It's like the time I need to relax enough to be dragged into dreams goes up and down, backwards and forwards like the waves outside my window. I also make a tiny boat from paper and it casts a shadow on my crooked walls. It looks like a huge ghostly galleon sailing against a grey sky. I watch the rainbows glow softly and I worry about tomorrow and Ceto Class and what they saw.

In the morning Mum gives me a big hug and tells me I'm brilliant and I lean into the warmth of her and I feel the baby kick between us. It's kind of amazing and kind of terrifying. I wonder how something that hangs in a space between life and death and who is a question mark in our future can make such a ripple.

The baby is all alone in the dark and still wants to be known.

Mum gives me a pair of monkey slippers just like Cameron's and sometimes I think she must be able to read my mind. Other times I know I fold things away so carefully that there's no way she could ever know and that's how I want it.

I put the slippers carefully into my book bag and I sit at the table and eat toast and peanut butter. Zofia is spreading Marmite on her toast so thickly that I think she must have confused it with Nutella but she inhales it in five seconds flat. Then she has another round just the same. *Shall we do the boat tonight* she asks and I nod because the thought of the boat is like a bright light in the gloom of the day. The glue will have set by tonight and I start making a list in my head of all the things we can do next and the thoughts of Ceto Class are pushed out and away.

Tom walks. Very. Very. Very. Slowly. I think I deserve a medal or at least a certificate for not shoving him into the sea because people walking slowly when they could be running or jumping or sprinting or skipping or cartwheeling is one of the most annoying things in the whole world. I give him some hard stares and a growl and finally I shriek *will you please move you absolute snail* and he trots forward like a shy pony.

Ceto Class are hopscotching again in the playground because Mo is convinced he is in with a chance at a world record. Everyone is crowded round and cheering and we've clearly missed something important because of Tortoise Tom. I race over but he hangs back and when I look down his fingers are dancing by his sides. I shout *come on slowpoke* and Cameron turns round and says *yeah come on slowpoke. Mo just did a whole game in two minutes thirty-five* which is apparently only about triple the world record.

TOM

No one is laughing at me. No one is skirting around my edges and leaving me in my own space. Alone. No one is pointing or whispering behind their hands. No one is throwing words at me like freak or pathetic or scaredy-cat or worse. No one is acting like a single tiny thing has changed. But I feel like someone has peeled off all of my layers and on that day on Nathan's boat everyone saw right inside me. They know. Before I could just be Tom and no one knew and now they do. And I can't change that and now I will always be the scared pathetic boy just like Dad said.

Everything has changed. I slip in beside Cameron but my heart is thundering towards my shoes.

For days all we do is boat. Boat boat boat boat boat. I don't have time to practise underwater breathing or swimming because it's just boat this, boat that. The measuring parts are really tedious and apparently really important and obviously Tom absolutely loves it. He and the tape measure are practically best friends. He probably sleeps with it under his pillow. He's probably given it a name. Mike or Gary. Maybe Trevor. Trevor the Tape Measure.

It's starting to look more boaty. We've just turned it over so we can stick the hull on to it and it's definitely more promising than Dad's first attempt. Not that he's been very involved, which is probably why. He said he'd help us but actually he's been too busy doing boring things in the house or boring things at work. The things in the house are all to do with the stupid baby but I don't ask for details because it makes my heart squeeze.

Tom stays in the stables doing some measuring and I wander inside. Fiona is folding tiny little onesies in the living room and suddenly I feel like I'm trying to swim to Fiji and jellyfish are crawling over my skin and the sea is in my lungs which is absolutely ridiculous because I am standing on dry land in a house.

Fiona sees me staring and instead of asking something boring like if I want to help she goes and gets us both milkshakes and she sits down on the sofa and asks if I'd like to watch a Ghibli film with her. She says she's never seen one before and I can't quite believe it so I put on *Howl's Moving Castle* because it's my favourite. We sit together but not too close together and we watch the film in the quiet and when it's over she says it's one of the best things she's ever watched.

TOM

There are still two months to go until they want to deliver the baby but the room is nearly ready anyway. Mum and I stick glowing stars on the ceiling just like in my room and I like the idea that we have the same light. Mum keeps looking at the room and saying that there's something's missing. *Yes, the baby* I say and my heart nearly stops because what if the baby is always missing? But she laughs and spins the mobile with her finger so the birds fly in frantic circles. She puts her hand on her tummy and she looks so tired that I help her put away the tiny white sleepsuits into the chest of drawers. Some of them are stitched with stars and moons and some of them have tiny sea-creature patterns and one has clouds and lightning and rain and rainbows. I like that one a lot. It looks so impossibly small and I remember Mrs

Adams's yellow hat so I run to my room and get it. I give it to Mum and she says *oh it matches the walls perfectly* and *isn't it so tiny* and I nod and I think I feel excited.

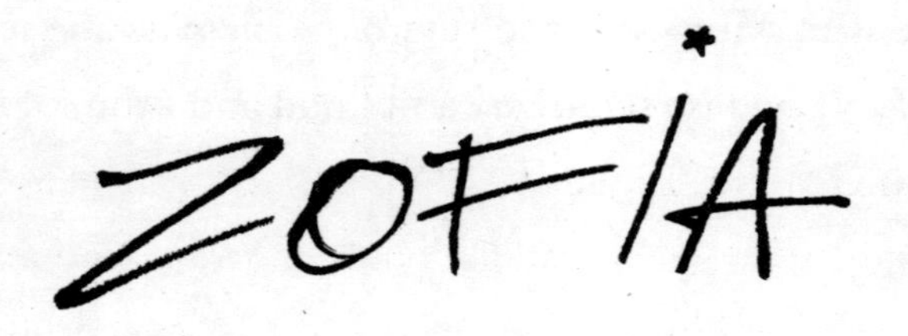

Dommo and I fly her kite together. There isn't really enough wind so what happens is I run really really fast holding the string and she throws the kite up in the air and the bird-shape dances in the sky for three or four seconds and then lands on one of our heads. Then we grab our wetsuits and scramble into the sea and kick our way towards Fiji but we're laughing and splashing and I don't care that we're not going to make it. I tumble and spin and the icy water doesn't freeze my limbs. By the time we stagger out on to the sand we're blue-lipped and shivering but instead I feel warm.

I haven't thought about the baby or Tom or Fiona all afternoon.

TOM

Mum and I play Mario Kart for most of the afternoon. It's actually Zofia's game and I'm worried because we haven't asked her and she's at the beach again but Marek says it's fine. I'm a funny raccoon creature and Mum is a mushroomy thing and we race around strange bendy tracks and throw shells at each other and at first I'm not very good but my fingers learn the right way to move just like they do in origami. I skid round corners and get big boosts that push me over the finish line and Mum comes last every time. She doesn't mind though.

Then we hear a thump and a crash and all the noises Zofia makes when she comes home. She comes into the living room after having a shower and I think she'll shout at us for playing her game. She looks at the screen and says *Fiona, have you lost every single time, that's like some sort of record* and Mum laughs. Zofia gets another controller and she sits next to Mum and shows her how to get the big boosts and some special shortcuts and she doesn't get cross when Mum forgets which button to press or when she falls off the track instead of jumping. She just shows her again and claps her hands with glee when Mum manages to spin into first place against me. Then we all race together and Zofia and I battle for first place and she wins one and I win two. In the final race Mum slips ahead of both of us at the last moment and she cheers and does a victory dance that makes me and Zofia laugh our heads off.

Mum and Marek start to make supper together and Zofia and I wander out to the stables and saw some wood for the boat and just for a moment everything feels just like I think a proper family should.

Just for a while.

ZOFIA

When the school secretary pops her head into the classroom during double maths and asks me and Tom to come with her I do a little dance in my head and then in real life too. Missing double maths because Dad forgot to send back that form about the school trip when we're going fossil hunting or to send in lunch money or even if we have to have a nit check is the best thing ever. I skip down the corridor and practise my hopscotch footwork because Mo is getting a bit too loud about being better than all the girls. Tom does his usual tortoise walk and if I didn't know him then I'd think maybe he was trying to drag out the time away from maths. But he loves maths. I turn back to him and his face is paper-pale and his hands are doing that strange fluttering thing again. Worry worry worry.

It's just a forgotten form I hiss and he doesn't look any happier. Maybe late forms are a really big deal for him.

TOM

It's that moment again. That heartbeat of quiet before the explosion. I can sense it curling around me like a cold wind.

I've done this walk before. I've done it when Dad hurt Mum. I've done it when we ran away and Mum came to collect me in secret. I've done it when Dad was arrested. I've done it when Dad was sent to prison and they told me he wasn't going to be allowed out for a long time. That was the last time I did the walk and it was at my last school but it is still the same. It always starts with being scooped out of the classroom and everyone staring and whispering. Then walking through corridors that buzz with silence because everyone else is in their classrooms doing normal things like normal children. Then getting to go in the headteacher's office which is almost special but it's too scary. Then sitting on scratchy chairs. Then quiet gentle voices saying words that land as heavy as iron.

Zofia doesn't know but I do. Something terrible has happened and she is skipping ahead and calling for me. I don't want to walk any faster. I don't want to walk towards the words that will change everything.

ZOFIA

Ms Laghari is sitting behind her desk in her office and I haven't been in here before when I haven't absolutely known I was in trouble. I still think that Leo was stupid to believe that rice pudding was actually frogspawn and he didn't have to be sick all over the lunch table either. And Dommo and I didn't mean to redecorate the art room when we learned about a painter called Jackson Pollock and thought we'd be able to make one of his pictures easy-peasy. But Ms Laghari doesn't look like she did then. She says *sit down, sit down, you two. Now there's something I have to tell you* and I can suddenly feel jellyfish on my skin.

TOM

We don't get to go to the hospital straightaway. Dommo's mother picks us up and we go back to nearly home but it's next door. Dommo's cottage is busier than ours. There are paintings on every single sloping wall and plants that burst from pots and trail from shelves. We couldn't stay at school because of our family emergency but we couldn't go home because of it either. So we sit and Zofia eats Oreos like her whole life depends on it and I watch the steam rising from the sugary tea Dommo's mum says I need but that I can't swallow.

It's like the whole world has been carried away on the seatide. It's so small and far away and we've been left behind. Just me and Zofia and Dommo's mum and Pablo alone at the end of the universe.

We sit and wait for news. It's the most terrifying

time and somehow it's also boring. The snaking panic in my bones can't keep up its biting and slithering for this many hours. It tries its best and my breath is sharp and short and my fingers tremble and I fold a piece of newspaper into a square without thinking. My fingers follow the familiar lines and sharp folds. I feel a rise of panic and guilt. This is what I should have been making the cranes for all along. From the moment I heard. But I was selfish and stupid and it's my fault that the baby was born so early and so poorly. I make the paper bird and then another and another. I can fix this. There's still time.

ZOFIA

I have eaten so many Oreos that I might be sick but then I'm not actually sure it's the Oreos that are making me feel like this. There's a drag of worry in the pit of my stomach and no matter how many biscuits I stuff into it I can't make the feeling go away. I keep thinking what if and how and what's happening and all the questions make me feel dizzy. They're layering themselves in my brain one on top of another until there's a mountain in my mind and my head hurts like it might burst. There's a gnawing inside me that feels like when I try to swim to Fiji but it's a thousand times worse and with every second that swishes past it grows and wriggles until I think it might push through my skin and turn me into a monster. I wished and I wished and I wished that the baby would go away. I wished it and now it might come true.

Tom is folding newspaper into a bird. I watch his fingers moving quickly and like a spell they make wings and a beak and a long sweep of neck and it's actually magic. He puts it on the coffee table and I reach for it and hold it up to the light. It has sharp creases and angles but it's also so delicate that it seems soft and feathered. Tom takes up another piece of paper and he says *in Japan they believe if you make a thousand paper cranes then you'll be granted a wish by the gods*. And he starts to fold with neat precise hands.

Show me how I say.

TOM

Zofia isn't very good at folding paper cranes. A few weeks ago that would have made me secretly very happy but today I don't feel a thing. Instead I show her again and again how to make the folds flat and straight and the right order to build a bird. She mutters darkly and her eyes flash in that dangerous way but I ignore it. I just keep folding the same lines and among a growing pile of screwed-up snowballs of paper she eventually produces a battered crane. It looks like it could do with a visit to the vet but she strokes its wonky head with her thumb and picks up another square of paper from the pile I've cut. I want to go next door and get my proper origami squares but I don't want to go into that empty house and see all that empty space. So we fold from imperfect newspaper squares and make imperfect cranes and try to get closer to an impossible wish.

ZOFIA

Making paper cranes is practically impossible. I can run and jump and sprint and swim and do six cartwheels in a go and I'm very close to perfecting my backflip but this is ridiculous. My fingers won't do what my brain tells them to and I keep crumpling the paper. Tom's folds and lines are sharp and straight and mine wobble and leave ragged edges behind. He shows me the same stages over and over and over again and it feels a bit like when we were teaching Pablo to sit. I stormed off a lot then. Tom doesn't do that and he just repeats the pattern with quick and nimble fingers and I grit my teeth and follow the folds. It takes about a million hours but a wonky broken-necked bird starts to bloom from the paper in my hands and it's pretty cool.

Dad rings just before Dommo's mum starts making tea. I know it's him even before the first *brrrring* has bounced off the stone walls and I leap up and grab the phone and say *Dad Dad what's going on* and I sound like a stranger and there's something like panic knotting around my words.

I listen and my fingers crush the paper crane in my hand and it lies crumpled in my palm and I feel sick. Then I pass the phone to Tom and sit on the sofa.

Fiona's OK. There's a baby. Two whole months early. Tiny. Breathing but very sick.

Her.

Her.

Her.

I have a sister.

I take another piece of paper and I fold the lines.

TOM

We stay the night at Dommo's house. She is very quiet when she comes home from school and she doesn't try to wrestle Zofia or suggest one of their rainy-day games that usually involve nearly breaking a leg. She sits with us on the sofa and we don't really have any words to say or share. She sees the scatter of birds on the coffee table and twirls one through her fingers and she's so quick that it looks like it's flying. I pick up a square of paper and hold it out to her and Zofia and I show her how to make the cranes. She picks it up faster than Zofia did and I worry that might make Zofia storm off but she doesn't even seem to notice. We sit in a silence that wraps around us as the night steals the sun and we fold paper cranes.

That night I sleep on the sofa with all the lights on

and Zofia sleeps in Dommo's room. At 3 a.m. I hear a padpadpad of feet and I sit up with a thundering heart and a dry mouth. Pablo is next to me on the floor and his tail wags and he's not a very good guard dog. I put my hand in his curly fur and feel his reassuring warmth.

Zofia's wild-haired head sticks itself round the door and my pulse drops down to my toes in a whoosh of relief. *I can't sleep do you want a cup of cocoa* she asks and I nod and don't say a word. Her head disappears and five minutes later the whole of her reappears holding two china mugs patterned with polka dots. The sides are dribbled with sticky cocoa and more slops over as she hands me mine but I don't care. I take a sip and it's delicious and Zofia and I sit on the sofa. She is curled up like a cat and she's so quiet and she's so still. I think I can see tears sliding down her face but she brushes them away so fiercely that I don't dare say a word. I look at her and for the first time I see something fragile blurring her hard edges and for the first time I think maybe she isn't OK all the time. She's scared. And I know how that feels.

Zofia rubs her face and looks away from me and then she says *why are all the lights on?*

And suddenly I'm so tired of keeping everything inside me. All of the fear and the worry and the secrets I keep folded up. I want to let them out and I want to tell this scared, still Zofia.

So I tell her. I tell her that Dad used to hurt us and now he's in prison but I'm still afraid and I tell her that he used to lock me in the dark when I was bad which was always and I tell her I didn't protect Mum and how every day I was so scared we'd go back to living how we did before. I tell her I can't sleep in the dark and how I can't keep out the black. How it creeps into my room and into my brain and it never leaves no matter how many lights I leave on. How it crawls up through the floor. How the dark gets in.

I tell her how I started folding paper cranes because I wanted to make a wish. I tell her I could have been making the cranes for the baby but I wasn't. I don't tell her what I was wishing for instead though.

When Tom tells me about everything that's happened to him my brain lurches me back to that moment when I locked him in the deep dark belly of the boat and I feel sick. I didn't mean to. I didn't know. But I still did it. I don't tell him but I feel it settling on my shoulders like a piece of granite and it's sinking me into the ground. I wish I'd known. But why would he have told me?

I remember the way Cameron looked at me when he saw me laughing at Tom on Nathan's boat. I remember the pure lightning bolts of fear that were flashing across Tom's face. I remember the thousands of lights dotted and hung and glimmering in his bedroom. I understand why he's so afraid. I understand why he carries light with him and why his fingers shake and why he makes a thousand paper shapes. Things start to slot into place like a jigsaw puzzle and I don't like the way I fit into the picture.

I feel a little cracked open. Like before I had a hard shell coating my skin and now it is starting to fracture and spidery lines are skittering across my surface. I look down at my hands and I feel I have to give something back to him because of everything of himself that he's just given to me. I twist my fingers round each other and I whisper *there's something wrong with me too. I can't swim to Fiji and every time I try it feels like I'm falling to pieces.* And then I say the really big huge thing that is niggling away and hiding in the dark spaces of my brain. *I wished the baby would go away. I wished it on the waves and it's come true. The baby being ill it's my fault. I did. I just … I just* and I'm trying to say what I feel but the words won't take shape.

Tom shakes his head no and he says *it's not your fault it's not your fault, we all say things we don't really mean* and he goes a little pink and he whispers *I wished for you to go away.* I almost laugh at his wish and my wish and the whole sad stupid mess we're in. *We can make it OK* I say back and I know we can. We sit on the sofa together until the morning light stretches its fingers through the windows. We don't say very much and at one point I fall asleep and topple sideways into Pablo who licks the inside of my ear. But we sit together and we wait.

TOM

I feel strange. I don't really know why I told Zofia all of that. I never ever wanted to tell her. I thought she'd laugh and point and scream to everyone at school what a weirdo I was – what a freak. That all her bouncing loud furious energy would ping back into her and something inside me would flicker in fear. But in the strangeness of the half-moon night and the silence, it happened. She didn't laugh. Her face changed in a way I didn't understand and she didn't look like Zofia for a moment. And then she opened her mouth and her voice was a whisper. And she told me all the dark and difficult things in her head and she sat with me all night on the sofa. I remembered what Mum had said about how Zofia was scared. And I understood.

In the morning she grabbed my hand just for a moment and she squeezed it.

Dommo's mum takes us to the hospital after she's nipped next door to feed Frida and nipped back to feed us. Dommo wants to come too and I'm not sure if I want her to or not but I don't get to make the decision because her mum says *no way, get to school, scamp* and Dommo hugs me and whispers *I wish you'd told me the baby was going to be born poorly* and I wish I had too because all the bad feelings have been trapped inside me for so long. Dommo squeezes me extra tight and then she hugs Tom and huffs off down the path to school.

We sit in silence in the car and the world whooshes by but it feels very far away. Tom goes his usual shade of light green but he doesn't throw up and I'm extremely glad because I'm sharing the backseat with him. I am still feeling strange and sick and heavy and actually I'm extremely glad I'm not sick either. Dommo's mum's car is quite nice.

She takes us where we need to be and it involves two lifts and one flight of stairs after the second lift went to the wrong place and then a thousand corridors. This is the hospital where Dad works but I hardly ever come here and it's another strange thing to add to the pile of strange things that's been building over the past day and night. We finally reach some double doors and Dommo's mum presses a bell to get someone to come and open them but before she can touch it Dad walks out and suddenly I'm wrapped up in his arms and my tummy settles and my skin stops stinging and my heart is less sore.

We go through the first set of doors and leave Dommo's mum behind on a plastic chair in the corridor. There's one more set and they say **Welcome to NICU** in rainbow-bright letters and there are cut-outs of little baby footprints stuck to the glass. Some of them are not even as big as my little finger.

And then there she is. Inside a big plastic box like a flopful fish stranded in a lonely tank. And she is tiny. I lean forward and I gasp at the smallness of her. Starfish hands and nails like seashells and arms and legs curled up like a frog's and snaked with wires. Her face surprises me because it's wrinkled and the baby is brand new but there's something magical about it all the same. I want to keep looking at her and I want to see if I can spot me or Dad in the roll of her cheek or the shape of her mouth. There's a tube disappearing into one nostril and a second tube that dips into her mouth. She opens her eyes and they're storm-dark blue and blinking. I can't stop staring. She's a whole person just waiting to unfurl. There's a starburst inside her waiting to explode and make her who she is and I want to know.

I reach out my finger and look at Dad to make sure it's OK and he nods so I touch the palm of her hand and she's velvet but I'm too rough and her sleepy face scrunches and I step back so quickly I knock over a plastic chair with a bang and everyone stares.

TOM

Mum is coming back down from the ward Marek tells me as I step inside the hot little room where my baby sister is. *She just went up for some painkillers and she'll be right down, OK?* I nod and then I look at the plastic box that Zofia is staring into without moving a single muscle. I've never seen her look at anything in the same way. All of her sharpness and her spring-loaded fury and bounce and energy have dissolved and she's hypnotised by the tiny baby in the box. She's so quiet and so still but when I walk forward she suddenly jumps back and knocks over a chair. The baby moves ever so slightly and Zofia storms past me and out through the double doors with a whoosh and a clang.

I look into the box. Light streams through it and paints rainbows on the white walls. The baby has a whisper of dark hair and you can see the trace of her veins and the tiny creases on her fingers. Her heart-beat makes her paper skin jump. Her feet are carved in miniature. Her hands are flowerfists furling and unfurling their pink petals. I put my finger through one of the round holes in the side of the box and I stroke her soft cheek and the meowing stops and I look at my sister. *You're astonishing* I whisper to the curl of her mouse-pink ear.

Then there is an arm around me kind and gentle but I still startle but the baby doesn't move. Her eyes are closed and she's so still I can see the jump of her heart in her chest. *I've missed you* says Mum and I hug her carefully because Marek said she was sore but I don't let go until my ragged edges have sewn to hers. *She's so calm now you're here* whispers Mum and we stay sewn together and watch the baby's chest rise and fall like the sea.

And just like that all the whole dark night spent in the light together is vanished from between us. I look through the double doors and I can see them all together. Tom stands with Fiona and Dad moves over to be with them and they're staring at the baby like it's the best thing in the whole entire planet and all my funny fizzing feelings when I saw her stormy eyes evaporate into the sharply disinfected air.

The baby doesn't like me. I'm too rough and too loud and Tom is gentle and soft and quiet and the baby is too and I heard what Fiona said to him. *She's so calm now you're here.* I suddenly can't stand being anywhere near this stupid happy family and I spin on my heel and I walk out through the next set of double doors and into the corridor.

Dommo's mum is sitting on a plastic chair reading

a magazine that's older than I am. She smiles at me and says *everything all right, love? I just saw Fiona heading in, poor woman is exhausted* and I feel the tempest stirring in my belly. I growl and I clench my fists and I try to breathe away the storm and Dommo's mum keeps talking and I want her to shut up. *Poor baby needs an operation, she's a poorly little mite and so small, even for being that early. What was she like, what did you think of your sister?* And I clamp my jaw to stop the thunder booming out and I don't say a word. Dad hasn't even come out to see where I am and I feel suddenly very very alone because Dad has another daughter now.

TOM

I stay with the baby for as long as I'm allowed. I marvel at her. I have a sister. I keep repeating it because it doesn't feel true. I have a sister. She's got dark eyelashes and crinkled ears and peach-soft cheeks. She is astonishing.

She is poorly. *Very poorly* says Marek and his lilting voice catches on the last word and cracks it in two. She needs her operation as soon as possible. The idea of someone with a sharp blade cutting into my sister's pink petal skin makes me want to cry. I want someone to tell me she'll be OK but no one can and so no one does and I sit with my sister and I whisper it to her instead. *You'll be OK*. I sit with my sister and I fold careful paper cranes and I tell her she'll be OK.

ZOFIA

We stay at Dommo's again that night. Dommo has about a million questions that I don't know how to answer about how the baby looks and how the baby is feeling and when the baby can come home. Tom says the baby is *astonishing* which is actually exactly right but I will never ever ever tell him. Dommo says she remembers when she was only three and her smelly little brother was born and how he looked like a little alien and she'd cried. Ted is now nearly eight and he has a snub nose and sandy hair and he looks absolutely nothing like an alien and absolutely nothing like Dommo or her mum either. She likes to tell him he was found on the beach as a baby all wrapped up in seaweed and no one else would have him so they ended up taking him home in a Tesco bag. She also says that being found on the beach means he's probably at least half sea cucumber which fits because he's revolting. He's currently making disgusting noises using his cupped hand in his armpit and so I shove him off the sofa. He sticks his tongue out at me and makes the noise again. I like Ted a lot. He's a proper brother.

Tom is all tense and white with worry but the thread that stretched between us last night has snapped. I don't ask him anything and he doesn't say anything to me. He is methodically folding paper cranes and Dommo is helping him and the living room is starting to look like a bird sanctuary. I don't make any. I'm not part of that any more.

TOM

The next morning we have to go back to school. It feels wrong. Everything is so different now but school is still waiting. Mum rings before breakfast and she sounds sad and faraway. The baby needed more help breathing in the night. I think of her all alone in the dark and my heart lurches even though I know she wasn't alone and she wasn't in the dark but in the warm glow of the incubator lights. I wonder if she's frightened. She still doesn't have a name and I want to give her one and make her permanent and stitched to us but I can't think of a single thing that fits her. Nothing is the right size or shape or sound.

Dommo and Zofia and I walk into the playground and Cameron and Leo rush over straightaway and the rest of Ceto follows. Cameron has made a card for the baby and he's drawn a picture of the beach on the front. I didn't know he could draw but he really can and it's bright with seaglow light. I give him a hug and I tuck it carefully into the pages of my writing book. I can show it to the baby this afternoon and tell her all about the sea and the sky and the wind and the salt and all the beautiful things she hasn't seen yet.

The day drags on and on. I don't listen to a word Miss Cassidy says and I run around the playground like a mad thing during break playing tag. I am the fastest and the loudest and I win win win every time.

After school Tom goes to the hospital and I go to the beach with Dommo and the rest of Ceto Class. Dommo's mum gives Tom a lift from school and she says *are you sure you don't want to come, Zofia* and I shake my head and I run to the beach so fast that the sand and pebbles spray up behind me in a gritty tornado.

It doesn't feel right. The sky and the sea are light and clear and warm air curls around me. It's a perfect beach afternoon. But I don't feel right. I don't want to play volleyball. I don't want to wrestle Leo. I don't want to write my name in the sand in letters so big they can be seen from space. I don't even want to swim but I try anyway because the water used to make things right. I rush into the water and I let the waves pull me off my feet and I fight against the current and the suck and the swash of the sea. But every time a wave crashes over my head I see them again. I see the three of them staring into the plastic incubator. I see four of them sitting round the kitchen table laughing together without me. I see three of them sitting sadly somewhere in the pages of the future and I'm not in that picture either. In either version I've been left behind.

I don't even try to get to Fiji. I drag myself back to shore and sit on the damp sand and surrounded by all of my best friends I feel alone.

TOM

The baby seems even smaller today. The tube in her mouth is pumping air into her tiny acorn lungs and she doesn't open her eyes. The rose-pink of her cheeks has faded to a snowy bloom. I'm not allowed to touch her. I whisper to her instead and I tell her not to be scared. I tell her to be brave even though I'm not. I run out of ways to tell her that so I tell her about my day at school. I show her Cameron's card even though her eyes are tight shut. I put it on the window sill next to her box so she can see the sea when she's ready. I touch the top of her box and I don't say goodbye. I whisper that I'll see her soon.

Mum is tired and her eyes are bright and pink-rimmed. She tells me how proud she is of me and she suggests names for the baby but I don't like any of them. I remember Marek suggesting Bathtap and

Xanadu and I offer them and Mum laughs and it's the best sound in the world. *Baby Bathtap* she says and she wipes her eyes. They're tears that are happy and sad which doesn't sound like it could happen but it does. When I have to leave I give Mum the tightest hug I can manage and she tells me I'm good.

Marek drives me back from the hospital. He can't live at the hospital with the baby like Mum can and he has to come home and do boring things that don't go away just because your baby is ill. I don't ask him if the baby is going to be OK because I don't want to hear one of the answers. He says the operation will last hours but they don't know when it will happen yet.

When we get home I head into the stables and I pick up a saw and I cut and plane and sand and glue. The boat shape is starting to emerge from the great flat sheets of wood and it's almost like magic. I spend hours and hours in the stables. I keep going even when I know I'll have to walk through the dark to the house. I keep going even when my tummy rumbles and Marek calls that supper is ready. I keep going even when Marek puts my plate on the workbench and slips away silently. I keep going until my lasagne is cold and the boat is nearly finished.

Dad tries to get me to go and help Tom with the boat but obviously I won't. He's taken that from me too. It was meant to be a joint project and he slipped into the stables like a quiet cat and didn't even think to ask if I wanted to do it as well.

Instead of building a boat Dad and I sit down for dinner. I trace my upside-down Z name on our table and it feels like there's been a million moments since we were last eating together just the two of us. Dad tells me the baby is more poorly and the hospital has decided the operation is happening early next week. There are just a handful of days left until we'll know whether she can stay for good. He tells me about how she arrived in a rush and how he barely got Fiona to the hospital in time and how when the baby arrived she cried right away and she sounded just like Frida and even though it had all been a stress and a worry he and Fiona had laughed anyway. I push my lasagne around my plate and nod like I'm listening really carefully but I don't ask any questions. Dad looks at me very hard with tired eyes but I don't look back. I have him all to myself for the first time in forever and there's a great gaping yawning snarling space between us and I can't fill it with words or noise and I don't know what to do. I wished for something awful and it came true.

TOM

I want to talk to Zofia. I want to rebuild those moments between us that happened in the tiny hours of the morning when we were both afraid. I want to tell her I am afraid that the baby will never have a name. I want to tell her that the operation is so big and the baby is so small. I want to tell her how scared I am that the baby will die.

I have friends at school to talk to and that's new and it's amazing. But there was something different about the way we talked together when there was no one else who understood except each other. But she won't talk to me now. She won't even look at me. At school she is her usual loud brash storm of herself but none of it is for me. She plays volleyball on the beach when I go and see the baby and she arrives home soaking wet and sandy and silent. We've spiralled and spun all the way back to when I first met her and there was nothing but fury in her.

The next day I work on the boat after school and after I see the baby. And again the next day. Zofia doesn't help me. I hope maybe she'll stick her head through the stable doors and she and Pablo will come bounding in and she'll pick up the wrong saw and the wrong wood and just get stuck in. But she doesn't. So I build it for us anyway.

The weekend arrives too quickly and too slowly all at once and I still haven't been to see the nameless baby or swum to Fiji or spoken to Tom or really spoken to Dad. I am a permanent stormcloud and I can't do anything about it and I don't understand it and I don't like it very much either. The thunder in me doesn't belong to me any more.

Dad goes to the hospital and I don't want to go. He doesn't push me and he just says *don't forget to feed the cat* and *today you live at Dommo's, so you can't set fire to anything, all right* and he sounds like my old Dad and I almost smile at him and he gives me a small hug but it doesn't hold me together like it used to do.

I slope down to the beach with Pablo and not with Dommo because I want a bit of peace and a bit of quiet which isn't like me at all. I dig a groove in the sand to sit in and I stretch my legs out towards the sea. The waves are glazed blue and lazy. Any other day and I would rush into the water and thrash my arms and legs against the current and spit the sea into the sky and gulp down the salty air and try and try to get to Fiji. But I just don't feel the fire today. I can't get there. I can't drag Dad down to the shore and point into the hazy distance and show him my orange flag flickering in the breeze next to his so he'll be proud of me. I can't do it.

I kick the sand and it dusts the air and gets in my eyes and I rub them and they stream and itch and I roar at the waves. The sound bounces off the clouds. I clench my fists and pound them into the beach and I keep doing it until the grains are spiking under my fingernails and I feel raw knuckled but a little better.

There's a strange noise. It's exactly like the sound a tea tray makes when it's been ridden down a flight of stairs covered in a duvet. A kind of whoosh and drag and thump and bump. I turn round and I squint against the bouncing light and I see Tom.

TOM

I tie a length of blue rope to the end of the boat. I looked up the knot I'd need and it was a bit like doing origami. I give it a tug and it holds firm. I finished the boat last night. The varnish has had twelve whole hours to stick and seal and dry and now the boat is a shining conker brown. It isn't perfect and I can already see things I'd do differently if I made one again but it looks like a boat and it looks like it'll float. I chuck the oars Saul gave us into the belly and tuck them under the rough wooden seat that stretches from one side to the other.

Then I drag. The boat is made from light wood but it is still tricky to navigate the twisty sandy stone-studded paths down to the beach. I have to stop and straighten the boat about fifteen times but once I reach the swoop of sand that bridges the curve of cliffs it's much easier.

There's someone sitting at the edge of the water. Even from this far back I can see the bright red of Zofia's pirate parrot T-shirt. I thought she'd be here. She's always here. I'm glad she is because I pulled and twisted and sweated to bring the boat to show her. She's hitting the sand and the air is filled with a sound I've never heard before. It's a cross between a roar and a wail. I stumble forward still holding the boat rope and she turns round and sees me. Her face is streaked with wet and her eyes are red-rimmed. I pull the boat closer to her and I say *Zofia, have you been crying* and she explodes.

How could he think I've been crying? I don't try to stop it. I don't try to breathe the clouds away. I don't care any more. I let the swirling storm burst out from me and I scream and I scream and I scream. *I'm not pathetic like you I'm not the one who can't stand the dark or loud noises or being away from my mummy or being locked downstairs on a boat for two seconds or being alone in the house that's you I am not like you I am not like you I am not like you.*

His face has gone oddly flat. His hands drop the blue rope attached to the boat he has been dragging down towards me. Then in words that are fluttering just below a whisper he says *what do you mean locked downstairs?*

TOM

My blood is ice and needles underneath my skin. There is a rushing in my ears and it's not the sound of the sea. It's something inside me. I haven't felt it before and I can't control it. I can't breathe it away. I can't count until it scuttles back to sleep. It ripples and it fizzes and it swirls. It's building into a hurricane.

Zofia locked me in the boat. I know it in a split-second lightning bolt of shock. It wasn't an accident. It wasn't a gust of wind blowing the door shut. It wasn't a mistake. It was her. She's just like George and Connor. She peeled back all my layers and showed Ceto Class the fear inside me that I try so hard to keep hidden. She showed Ceto Class how pathetic I am.

And suddenly I don't feel afraid any more. I don't feel the wriggle of panic in my spine. I don't feel the bright flash of fear fireworking in my brain. I feel something else.

I feel angry.

He roars. It's louder than me and it's louder than a lion and it's louder than the sea and the wind and the gulls. It rises around us and he is screaming at me.

He screams and his words hit me like rocks falling from the cliffs.

You are afraid all the time you're so afraid you can't even swim to that stupid rock you're afraid of the baby you're afraid of the change you're afraid no one loves you you're afraid you're afraid you're afraid and

I

hate

you.

The last three words are hurled like bombs and then he's ripping off his T-shirt and he flings it on to the sand and he's running towards the sea and he shouts into the stormy space between us but it's lost in the roar of blood in my ears and the whip of the wind and then he's under the waves.

TOM

The water is cold and it bites. The sea has been my light for months but it is dark now. It is nothing but forever blackness below me. The waves are rows of jagged teeth that tear and pull and nip. I kick my legs and struggle against the sea. It might be freezing but my blood is on fire. Fiji dips and bobs in and out of my vision as the water rises and falls and I try to keep my head up. I feel turned up and around just like when Zofia smashed me into the sand and the world spun. I can't keep track of where the sky is. But I can see the dark fringes of Fiji and I'm going to swim there. I haven't been in the sea since Dad and forever ago but I'm going to show Zofia. I'm going to show her that she can be afraid and I can be brave and that I can do what she can't and what she wants to do more than anything.

My anger keeps me afloat. Every time my muscles cramp and scream I think about the look on the Ceto boys' faces when the lights went on and they saw me. Zofia made that happen. And Fiji gets closer.

I am frozen and stuck in the sand. Tom has whooshed off into the sea like a shark wearing orange shorts and for a moment that's all I can focus on. A blur of orange and boy fighting against the waves and being swallowed by the sea.

Then the words that fell like rocks start to replay themselves in my ears.

He told me I was afraid.

And the jellyfish skin and the fury and the seawater lungs and the aching chest are all starting to fit into a picture. And I look at it.

And instead of feeling stormful and furious I feel

I feel

I feel

I can't find it. I can't find the feeling. But it's sitting there on my chest and it's glowing and growing.

I am grappling for the feeling and for the word and to click my final understanding into place when I realise I can't see Tom. There's no slice of orange in the sea. There's no flash of pale elbows breaking the waves. There's no dark head aiming like an arrow towards Fiji.

Nothing.

TOM

My legs aren't working.

My lungs aren't working.

My arms aren't working.

The sky is turning starry.

The sea is turning dark.

I am light as the salt air.

I am heavy as the windbeaten rocks.

I am

I am

I am

I see him. An orange dot. Fading into blue.

I have lightning inside me but it isn't my usual kind. It doesn't make me rage. It sparks and shoots. It makes me move as fast as light itself. It burns through my skin and I am alive with it. I run to the boat Tom has left angled in the sand. I push it with all the superstrength my storm has given me. I try to run alongside it until the water is up to my belly button and then I fling myself into the boat and grab the oars. I strike at the water and dash the waves and I try to remember the rhythm Nathan taught us all on the beach two summers ago. Pull and flick. Pull and flick. Pull and flick. The boat lurches and tilts and rolls. I keep going and I grip the oars tighter until my knuckles burst white and it feels like I'll never get there. But I have to. I have to.

And I do.

His head is still above the water but his arms and legs are twitching against the current like all the electricity has drained right out of him. I shout his name and I scream his name and he lifts his head and he says *help* and I have never seen a single movement and never heard a single sound that is better than that.

TOM

I try to grab the boat but it's too smooth and my fingers scrape down the hull. I can't pull myself up and out of the waves enough to grip the edges. Zofia leans half her body out of the boat and she holds out her hand and I reach for it. I miss twice and I am moved backwards and forwards by the grip of the sea. She wriggles and adjusts but when she catches my fingers in hers she can't pull me. I can't pull myself. I can't kick any more. Zofia doesn't let go. She holds my hand and she says *it's going to be OK* and I remember saying those words to the baby a few days ago. It feels like a moment from someone else's life being played in my mind.

Then she lets go.

I can't pull him up. For a birdboned boy he's too heavy with the weight of the ocean on top of him. I can't keep holding him like this forever, stuck in the sea and floating ever outwards and further from the shore.

I scrabble to the front of the boat, keeping myself low and flat to the floor so I don't tip it up. I plunge my hands into the water and stretch out my fingers until I find what I'm looking for and pull it to the surface.

The trailing blue rope Tom tied to the front so he could bring it to the beach. I try to pull it free but it's tied tight. I lean forward again and examine the knot with my fingers. I can imagine his quick careful fingers looping and tying so that the rope stayed stuck fast. I wish he'd made a mistake. But he hasn't. I tug at the blue rope heart at the centre of the tangle. I pull. I twist. I tear. It gets tighter. I start to growl inside my head and then I stop. It won't help. I have to think. I have to be careful.

I follow the lines of the rope with my finger. I can feel precious seconds slipping away and I turn to check Tom is still above water and kicking and he is and he's kicking gently to keep himself upright and he's so tired that his eyes are fading. I have to be quick and I have to be careful and I have to be calm even if inside I am howling.

I take a deep breath and I see the tail. I pull. And the knot releases.

TOM

Zofia is tying the blue rope around my chest. It rubs against my salt-damp skin and it burns but I don't cry out. I use the very last of my strength to help her tie a knot and then I wrap my fingers around the blue. And she pulls. And pulls. And pulls. And with a suck and a thwack I hit the side of the boat like a stunned bird and she grabs my hand and places it on the edge. *Slowly slowly careful* she whispers *don't tip the boat* and she helps me pull one leg and then the other and I land with a wet thump on the bottom of the boat.

And she looks down at me from the bench seat and she grins that wide Zofia grin and she starts to row to the shore.

I don't want to be a massive show-off but I basically just saved Tom's life and I should definitely have some sort of award ceremony and quite possibly a real gold medal. Or one made of chocolate. That might be more useful.

I pull the boat right on to the beach. I might need my arms amputating due to overuse. Pablo bounds up to us and he has no idea what's just happened because he's a dog and not a very clever one at that but he barks and licks the salt from my hands.

Tom sits up in the bottom of the boat. *Do you need a doctor* I ask and he shakes his head and he says *I was just tired I didn't go under I didn't swallow the water I'm OK but if you hadn't rowed out if you hadn't rowed out* and he can't finish his sentence because he's stuck on the moment just before something awful could have happened.

I sit next to him in the boat and I say *I like your boat it's very good at being a boat* and he gives me a tired grin and says *yeah thanks for all your help getting it finished*. I look at him like he's mad and I wonder if somehow the seawater went through his ears and into his brain and now all his thoughts are being washed with salt.

You did it all yourself you squirrelled yourself away in the stables and left me alone and there's a little edge of thunder in my voice. He looks at me like I'm the one with the salt-soaked thoughts and he says *I thought you would come if you wanted to and then you didn't so I thought you … you didn't want to do it with me any more.*

This is all so unbelievably stupid. I shrug my shoulders and put my arm over the side of the boat to scratch Pablo's ears.

What you said I begin and I try to make sure I have the words lined up before I say them so I don't make everything bad again. He starts to speak and he starts to say he's sorry and he didn't mean it and I shake my head fast and sprinkle the air with the sea. Because he was right.

TOM

Zofia lets an ocean tumble out of her and tells me how she is scared and how she's never had to share her dad before and how she hated having these two new people in her house and how she thought we were stealing her dad and that he liked me and Mum more and she feels like he is slipping further and further away from her and how the baby was all at once the best thing in the whole world and the worst thing because what if she died and what if she didn't and her dad loved the baby more than her and how she couldn't make her dad proud of her because she couldn't swim to Fiji and how she used to be brave and how she's just been so angry forever and it's harder and harder to breathe through the stormclouds.

I grab her hand just like she did for me that one

night in the light and I say *you just saved my whole life, Zofia* and she shrugs but there's a little gleam in her eye. I look down at her hand and I say *I wish I could be as brave as you I'm always so afraid* and she looks right back at me and says

Tom, you're the bravest person I know.

And he is. It's like I've had my head in the strange twisty briny deep of the sea and all the water and light and waves made me see everything upside down and back to front. Tom told me all about his dad and what happened to him and prison and I still didn't get it. But I do now.

Tom is the bravest person I know.

TOM

Marek isn't back from the hospital when we get to the cottage and I'm glad. Zofia and I have done a special complicated handshake that means we won't tell anyone what happened on the beach and in the sea today. We dragged the boat back to the stables together and locked the door behind us.

I have a very hot bath and get dressed in warm dry clothes and I feel so tired and cosy that it's hard to believe a few hours ago I was nearly at the bottom of the sea. It's hard to believe that a few hours ago I didn't believe Zofia and I had a single thing in common.

Zofia comes into my room still wet and smelling of the sea. She's holding a plastic bag and a hammer and at first I'm a bit afraid and very confused. But she just grins and kneels down. She pries up floorboards and she makes it look like she's done it a thousand times before. Which she probably has because she pulls out a tin of chocolates and offers me one. But then she opens the plastic bag and pulls out a long tangle of lights. *Christmas ones with batteries* she says and then she stuffs them under the boards. When she's finished putting the floor back together she hands me a remote and I press the button. And just like that, the darkness has nowhere to hide. Light dances through the cracks. It's pale and warm and beautiful. She listened. I start to speak but she's already disappeared into the bathroom.

While Zofia runs her bath and sings loudly and badly I get out my cardboard box. I sit on the sofa in the living room with Pablo and Frida and I open it and start to count.

That night I sleep in the dark, except for the glow of the light she gave me.

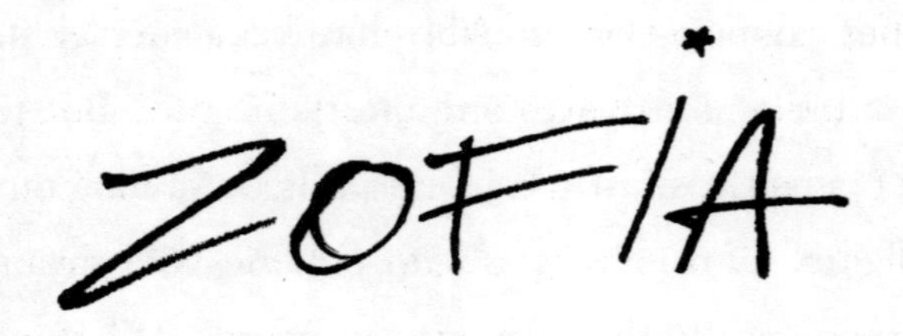

Dommo's mum takes Tom and me to see the baby together. I am afraid. I know that now. The tingly jellyfish skin and the seawater chest and the fizz of something inside is fear and it's panic and I have to know that because if I don't it'll never go away.

Dad is sitting by the baby and instead of feeling cross I feel safe. Dad is there with my sister. I go and stand by him and I put my arms around him and I hug him tighter than I've ever hugged anything. I want to make a joke about me being an anaconda but I decide it's not the best time. Instead I say *I'm sorry I wasn't good about the baby* and then I trail off and let the rest hang unsaid. He hugs me back just as tightly and he says in a voice full of the sea *you're my best fiercest first girl and I could never love you any less only ever more* and I bury my head in his shoulder.

The baby is still in her plastic box. She has a tube in her nose and one in her mouth and her eyes are closed. She is still extraordinary. Dad and Fiona go to get coffee and Tom and I sit either side of her cot. We tell her in whispers about our beach adventure because she can be part of our secret too. I think of her tiny lungs burning for every breath and I think she's like me underwater, stuck in a strange other world. She just needs to be brave and to keep trying. *Practise and you'll get stronger* I whisper. *I promise*. One of the nurses comes over to check a tube and he smiles and says *she's so calm with you two, good work, keep talking to her* and so we do.

I just want her to get better I whisper to Tom and he looks at me through the plastic box that holds our sister and he whispers back *so do I*.

There are three days before her big operation. And all we can do is hope. Hope hope hope.

TOM

It isn't very hard to organise everything I need to do. The day after the big rescue I check how many paper squares are left from my big Christmas present stash. I call Cameron and I go round to see Dommo and then they tell everyone else and the news spreads like a spiderweb through Ceto Class. In less than two hours everything is sorted and I am dashing about making sure we have enough biscuits and squash. Then I shout to Zofia to come with me and I lead her over to Dommo's.

Everyone from Ceto Class is squeezed into Dommo's living room. I give a demonstration and then Dommo sits with Halima and Mollie and Mo and I sit with Cameron and Jacob and Jude and Zofia sits with Leo and Alma. We show them exactly how to fold the lines and crease the paper until a bird emerges and its wings stretch out. I have four hundred and seven cranes in my box and I don't need them for me any more.

We need another five hundred and ninety-three before we can make our wish. And time is running out.

ZOFIA

Obviously we cannot make five hundred and ninety-three cranes in one afternoon. That would be completely ridiculous. Most of Ceto Class can't even make them at the start of the afternoon and they spend ages crumpling paper squares and saying rude words and getting hot and bothered. I feel a bit like Tom when I keep showing them all carefully and patiently even if it is quite boring and annoying.

At the end of the afternoon we have made eighty-two and I think most of those were probably Tom. Leo has made one and it looks like it was eaten by a cat and then thrown back up again and if Frida were about I'd suspect it had been.

But I grab great handfuls of paper squares as people are leaving to go home for tea and I say *keep going please keep going* because it feels very important and it feels like the only thing we can do. And we only have two days.

TOM

The baby's operation is tomorrow. We don't have enough cranes. I made them all night. I wasn't afraid for myself and I wasn't fighting the darkness. Every bird I folded flooded me with more and more light. More and more hope. But in the morning my fingerbones ache and my skin is raw and there still aren't enough.

But when Zofia and I arrive at school together people I don't know keep coming up to me and giving me paper cranes. They just drop them into the palm of my hand and say *good luck* and then they dissolve back to their classes and I'm left a bit stunned. Leo and Mollie have filled their schoolbags with them and so have Halima and Alma. Cameron and his dad stayed up late and he gives me a cardboard box that rustles with paper wings. Mo's mum has made fifteen yellow birds and Jacob and Jude give me a shopping bag from them and Nathan. Dommo gives me six and says she's working on number seven. I ask her how this has all happened and she shrugs and the tips of her ears turn red and she says *must be magic mustn't it*.

Miss Cassidy gives me ten perfect rose-pink cranes. Miss Laghari gives me five and they're patterned with beautiful tiny swirls and dots that she's drawn herself. The grumpy caretaker gives me a bag from him and his wife and his granddaughters who go to the big school now. The school nurse has made five blue-paper birds that look like they could really fly. The art teacher has made twenty because she already knew how and they're each a different colour.

They keep flooding in. Flock after flock. At home time parents line up in the playground and they've come in specially to give me handfuls of cranes and some of them are wonky and some of them are sharp but all of them are exactly how they should be. I have to borrow canvas bags from the school so we can take them home carefully packed. On the walk home I hear a shout and Zofia and I both jump and it's Saul from the boatyard and he says *here you are* in a voice so gruff I can barely understand each word and he gives me a wooden box. I open it and it's brimming with birds. They're so neat and straight and perfect that I gasp and he mutters something about it not being a big deal and he's always liked this sort of thing and he stomps off again very quickly. I can't imagine those big rough hands making these tiny delicate creatures but they have and I nearly cry.

As we walk up the path Dommo's mum rushes out with Ted and she's red-faced and embarrassed and she says *I tried my best, it's hard isn't it, Ted* and then she gives us a handful more.

We go home and we count. It takes a long time and Zofia gets hungry halfway through but we get there after Oreos and orange juice.

998.

And Zofia and I make one last crane each. Together.

It's the day of the baby's big operation and the morning is bright and clear and new.

It's just Ceto Class on the beach. Just like it was before and just like it will be after. Pablo is exploring rock pools and finding strands of seaweed of his very own. Dommo gives me a hug with such unexpected ferocity that I nearly fall over but instead I just cling to her with all my strength and I hug her back.

We stand on the edge of the water and we listen to the waves. We smell the salted sky and we watch the clouds curl. We are each holding a cardboard box full of paper cranes. Tom nods to me and I nod back and we all walk forward as one and we set our birds on the waves. A thousand paper cranes swim and flap and swirl and float and sink and rise and fall on the swell of the sea. They stretch their wings all along the gentle blue and the water is studded with bright jewels.

We watch them floating out towards the line where the sea meets the sky. The tide washes forwards and backwards and it can carry something to us or take it far away. Tom and I step back and Ceto Class follows. I hold out my hands and we all stand in a linked chain. And we close our eyes and we wish. A wish from all of us and for one of us. A wish that will wash away my wavewish and start something new and brilliant.

We wish.

Together.

TOM

I have not been looking forward to today an awful lot. It's our end-of-summer weekend for Ceto Class before we scatter across new forms at the big school in town. We'll learn to surf and bodyboard and duck-dive and sail. It's absolutely fine for someone like Zofia who is part fish. I'm all human boy and I'm nervous. But that's OK. I can cope with that much better than before.

I sit on the beach in my boat. Saul helped me smooth its edges and fix some of the rockscrapes from the rescue mission. He didn't ask what had happened and I didn't tell him but he did say in his funny gruff way that I'd done a good job of building a boat and I could come to the yard any time and he'd teach me a bit more.

Ceto Class starts to arrive. Leo races past and right into the sea in his clothes and Dommo calls him an absolute idiot and Cameron yells *I'm on your team for sandcastles* at me and just like that the day is started. Windsurfs and surfboards are laid out on the sand and there are the buckets and spades for the sandcastle-building competition. I might be good at that at least.

Zofia is stretching on the shoreline. She waves at me and grins and I wave back. Behind me I hear a noise but I don't jump and leave my skin behind. My new counsellor is helping me deal with that sort of thing much better. Her name is Jenny and she's kind. She's helped me understand the bad things and see that I'm safe now. I sleep in my room in the dark except for the cracks where the light gets in. I can see the light in everything. I don't have to squash and squeeze my own feelings deep down because I think it'll make Mum happy. I talk about them now. So does Zofia. We all keep each other safe.

Marek sits down next to me in his wetsuit and groans. *I think I'm too old and tired for this* he says with his voice like the waves and I say *yeah you probably are* and he gives me A Look and then he laughs and I do too.

Zofia shouts *come on you lazy thing get a move on* and he gets up and groans again and says *better follow orders, wish me luck* and I say *you'll need it at your age* and he aims an invisible bow and arrow at my head. He walks towards Zofia and links his arm through hers. They walk towards the sea together and start their swim. I can see Zofia's orange flag tied to her wetsuit and then Marek's blue one flashing in the sun.

Sorry I'm late, someone threw up all over their nice outfit says Mum and she sits down beside me on the sand and I reach out straightaway for Ula. A tiny perfect name for my tiny perfect sister. Ula Hope. Ula means sea jewel in Polish and it was Zofia's idea. It's just right. Hope was my idea. It's just right too.

Ula still has her night-dark hair and her seastorm eyes but she's bigger and louder now and I love her so much. She is a piece of me and a piece of Mum and a piece of Zofia and a piece of Marek and she is utterly herself. She loves the sea and she loves the starlight on her ceiling. She has a thin silvery-red thread of a scar that stitches itself across the top of her tummy and it's the last reminder of how close we were to losing her and how hard she fought to be right here now with us. Zofia calls it her shark bite and tells everyone she saved her sister from the snapping waves. But she didn't. She saved me.

I will teach Ula to be careful and thoughtful and brave because I'm good at being all of those things even if I didn't think so before. Zofia will teach Ula to be wild and quick and even braver because she is all of those things and a lot more. I know now that you can be loud and cross and *tempestuous* and also one of the kindest people in the whole world.

I put Ula on my lap and we sit in the boat together on the sand. I kiss the top of her head. She's wearing her knitted yellow hat and she smells like sugar and salt. I point at the sea and the sky and to Fiji and to Zofia and Marek swimming fast towards it to place their flags. *There's our sister* I say into her seashell ear and she grasps my finger tight.

Dad and I stand with our feet on Fiji, our flags flickering in the wind and marking out our space together. The sea was strong but I was stronger. He puts his arm around me and I lean into him and I feel the beat of my calm heart. I was born in a storm and I can still whirl myself into a tornado but I am learning to talk and listen instead of always becoming thunder.

I look back over the glittering sea at my family on the shore. A boy and a baby in a boat and a dog and a woman on the sand.

I stand on the ragged rocks of Fiji and I wave.

We made it. Together.

Helpful Organisations

Childline (NSPCC): childline.org.uk – a safe space for children to talk about anything they are going through with counsellors who offer a range of help and support, and advice on what to do if you are worried about a friend

Speak out Stay safe (NSPCC): learning.nspcc.org.uk/services/speak-out-stay-safe – an online safeguarding programme that helps children understand abuse in all its forms, children's rights to be safe, and the sources of help available so that they can speak out about abuse

Women's Aid/The Hideout: womensaid.org.uk and thehideout.org.uk – support women and children who have experienced or are experiencing domestic abuse, including information on what to do if you are worried about someone else

Refuge: refuge.org.uk/get-help-now/children – supports women, men, young people and children

Family Rights Group: frg.org.uk – promotes policies and practices that keep children safe within their family, and strengthens the family and community networks of children who cannot live at home

Children Heard and Seen: childrenheardandseen.co.uk – supports children, young people and their families who are impacted by parental imprisonment

Acknowledgements

Thanks as always to my brilliant team at Bloomsbury Children's – Beatrice, Jade, Fliss, Stephanie, Anna, Sarah, Michael – who have worked on each of my books with such kindness, patience and enthusiasm. Thank you to Sydney Smith, whose unrivalled talent is something I never dreamed would grace the cover of my book. Thank you too to everyone at Felicity Bryan Associates, especially my wonderful agent Catherine Clarke and the indefatigable Michele Topham.

Thanks to Leah Carden for talking me through plots and some very insightful title suggestions. Thank you to Ross Montgomery for being one of the first readers and for being a really excellent lockdown walking buddy. Thank you to the lovely Taz Subramanian for answering my many vague and uninformed questions about paediatric surgery.

Thank you to my parents – I've said it before but I really do owe you everything.

Thank you to my writerly friends (in particular Yasmin Rahman, who read this and helped so much when I was having a wobble) and to all the teachers, reviewers, bloggers, librarians and readers who have been so generous with their support.

Thanks as always to Patrick Simpson for being the kindest and most tolerant person on this earth, and also for not arguing when I said I was getting a puppy once I'd finished this book. I think you'll agree that despite the slightly gnawed look of our furniture, this was a good choice.

Finally to Lucy Mackay-Sim. Thank you for being the editor of my dreams, from that very first Quaver-filled meeting to this final book together. I am so lucky that, although you are no longer my editor, I get to go forward with you as my friend.

Turn the page for visual instructions of how to make your own paper crane ...

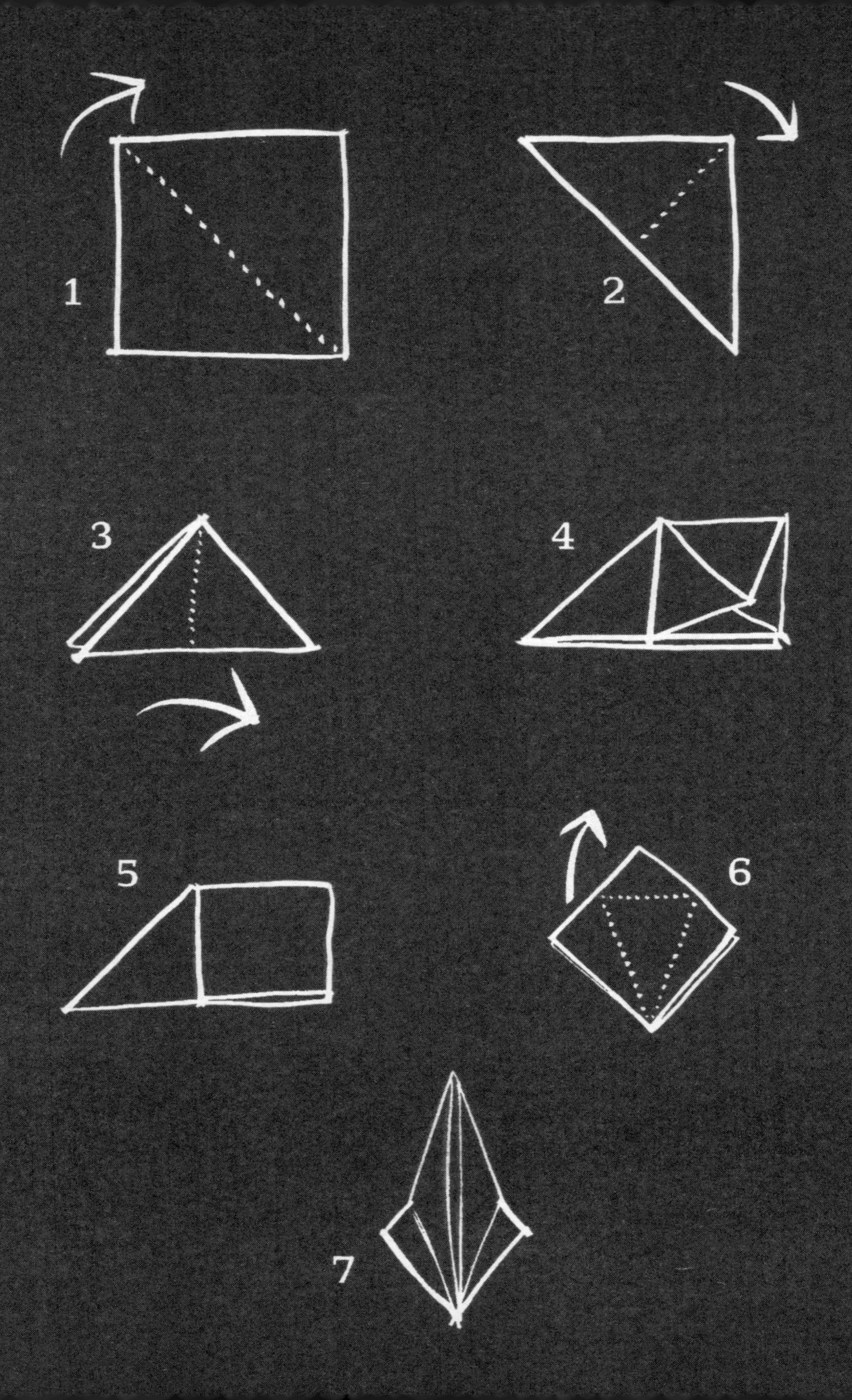
1
2
3
4
5
6
7

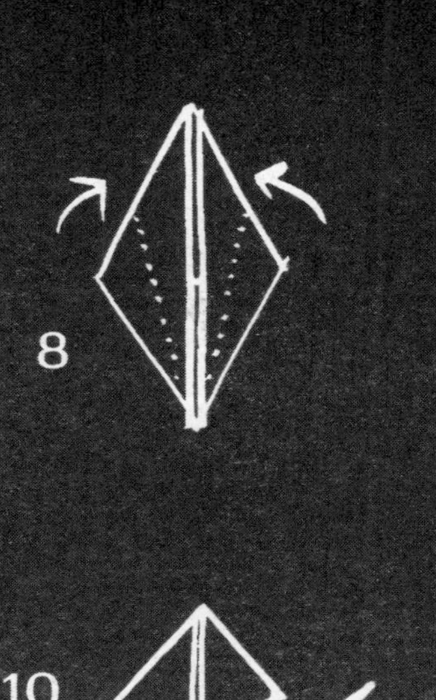
8

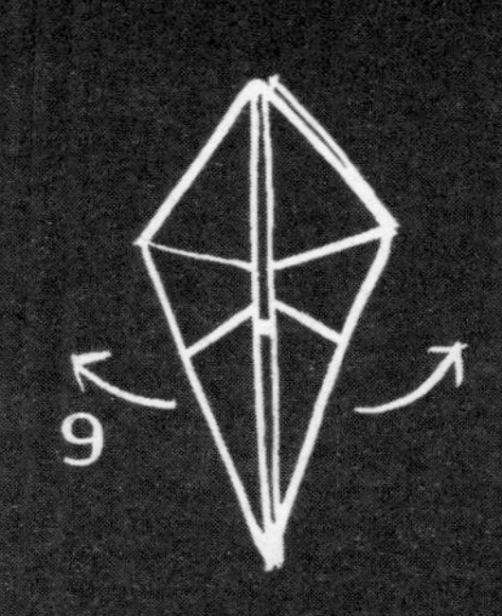
9

10

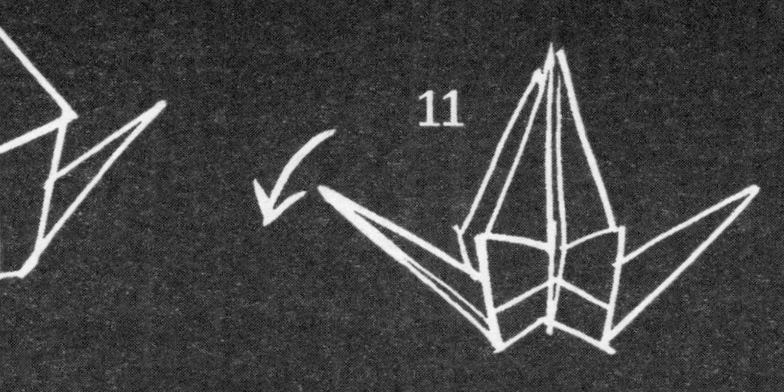
11

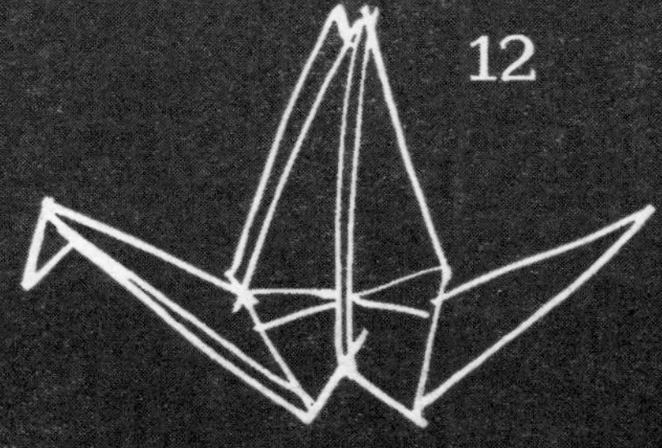
12

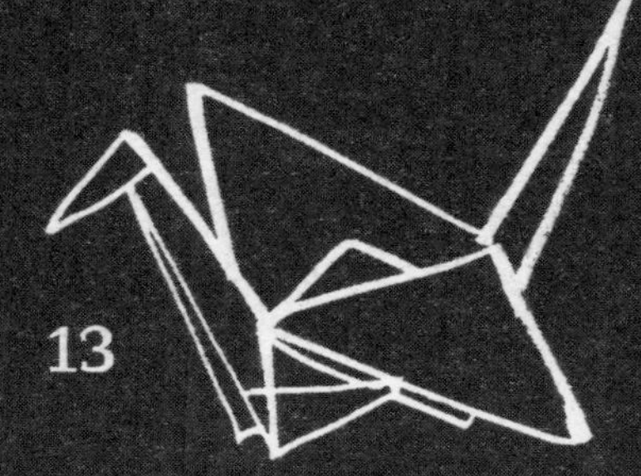
13

And also by Katya Balen

Winner of the Yoto Carnegie Medal 2022 and a classic in the making for anyone who ever longed to be WILD!

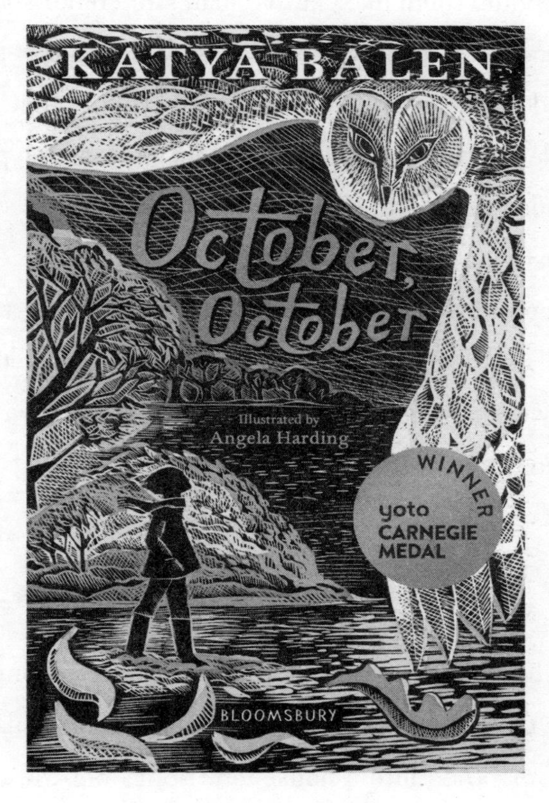

AVAILABLE NOW

Turn the page for a sneak peek ...

We live in the woods and we are wild.

Tonight we howl at the star-dusted sky. We throw our voices and shape them and mix them and mould them like clay. We can stretch our sounds so that they reach the very tops of our tallest trees and down to the secret-filled earth and so that they tangle in the brambles and skim across the pond because this world is ours and we are alone.

Just us.

A pocket of people in a pocket of a world that's small as a marble. We are tiny and we are everything and we are wild.

We live in the woods.

We live in the woods and we are wild.

Our house sits in the woods and it's made from the trees that frame it. They've been chopped and planed and smoothed into a house, and so it's not the same as looking at the twisted reaches of the branches but I like to be inside the woods. It feels like a secret because we are hidden away and forgotten about in the best way, even though people know we're here. We have to go into the village every year or so and buy the food we can't grow or the clothes we can't make, which is nearly all clothes except for socks and even those aren't very good when I try. Dad can turn a ball of wool into a foot shape with a click-clack of needles and half an eye on the stove but I can't manage more than a tangle. We get all the things we need for another year and slip back into the woods while the village forgets us again.

The house was built by Dad before I was born. I wasn't born here though, because at the last minute the woman who is my mother said *no way* and she was whisked off to the hospital and she was pushed down corridors that were white and bright and tree-less and blank and like nothing she remembered. But then she did remember. She remembered all the things like microwaves and internet and heating that happens at the push of a button and not from the roar of a stove that makes your clothes smell smoky and sweet. She remembered, and when she had her baby wrapped in a white blanket that matched the walls and the sheets and the pillows she said to Dad that she *couldn't go back*.

She did, for a bit. But she was floating off into the world that fringes ours, and when I was four she was gone. In my head I think I remember the day she left but the memory is like trying to hold water in my cupped hands and it trickles away before my eyes. There are wisps of a woman holding on to my hand and I feel my whole body being pulled along by the tide of another person running and my legs can't keep up. There's crying and I know that I let out a shriek so loud it pierced the sky and the birds scattered.

I wouldn't let her leave with me. I wouldn't leave the woods.